RESCUED BY THE MERMAN

JESSICA GRAYSON

ARIA WINTER

This is a work of fiction. Names, characters, businesses, places, events and incidents are either the products of the author's imagination or used in a fictitious manner. Any resemblance to actual persons, living or dead, or actual events is purely coincidental.

Published in the United States by Purple Fall Publishing. Purple Fall Publishing and the Purple Fall Publishing Logos are trademarks and/or registered trademarks of Purple Fall Publishing LLC.-
purplefallpublishing.com

Publisher's Cataloging-in-Publication data

Names: Grayson, Jessica, author. | Winter, Aria, author.

Title: Rescued by the merman : a Little Mermaid retelling / by Jessica Grayson and Aria Winter.

Description: Purple Fall Publishing, 2021.

Identifiers: ISBN:

978-1-64253-762-8 (paperback)

978-1-64253-706-2 (ebook)

Subjects: LCSH Mermen--Fiction. | Shapeshifting--Fiction. | Magic--Fiction. | Kings, queens, rulers, etc.--Fiction. | Princes--Fiction. | Fantasy. | Romance fiction. | BISAC FICTION / Fantasy / Paranormal | FICTION / Romance / Paranormal / General | FICTION / Romance / Paranormal / Shifters | FICTION / Romance / Paranormal / Witches | FICTION / Romance / Royalty | FICTION / Fantasy / Romance

Classification: PS3607 .R3978 R47 2021 | DDC 813.6--dc23

Cover Design by Kim Cunningham of Atlantis Book Design

PRINTED IN THE UNITED STATES OF AMERICA

DEDICATION

To my husband: You are not just my husband, you are my best friend and my rock. Thank you for all your love and support. I love you more than words can ever say.

-Jessica Grayson

PREFACE

HALLA

Every night, I dream of fire and chaos. Destruction and ruin. The Healers tell me the nightmares will fade over time, but I doubt this is true. I hold tightly to these memories because they remind me of when I was whole.

I dream of a man with eyes as blue as the northern sea. His hair is the color of the obsidian stone cliffs along the shoreline, and he studies me with a strange mixture of kindness and pity as my body floats, limp and broken, among the crashing waves.

He is my anchor in an ocean of pain as I feel myself drifting away on the sand. Reaching down, he gently strokes my cheek and whispers to me in the ancient tongue, "You must live, Princess Halla."

I awaken with a start. The fog of my nightmares recedes. Dark images retreat like tides from the shore, but one thing remains—my desire to find this strange man who saved me that day.

My brother insists he was a fever dream as I lay dying. An

angel conjured in my mind to help ease my pain and suffering. But when I close my eyes, I can still hear his deep voice and feel the whisper of his touch across my skin as he stared down at me.

"You must live, Princess Halla. You must live."

CHAPTER 1

HALLA

Fire and destruction rain down from the sky. The golden scales of the dragon glint in the sunlight as he flies overhead, releasing torrents of flame on our once proud city of Solwyck.

I watch from atop the castle as alarms blare throughout the streets, mixing with panicked screams in a cacophony of noise. The acrid smell of charred buildings and bodies chokes me. The fires of the city burn so hot, beads of perspiration cover my brow.

"Take my sword, Halla. It is made of L'omhara, the only metal that will pierce the dragon's scales. You must save the city."

My father's hand wraps around mine as he places the handle of the sword in my grip.

Tears sting my eyes and blur my vision as I reach down and cup his cheek. Ash falls all around us, whirling and dancing amidst the chaos like flakes of snow on the breeze.

"Father, you have to hold on. Please, you cannot die. I'm going to save you. I'm going to save us all."

"Where is Gerold?" he rasps. "Please, tell me he's not—"

"He's here, Father." My eyes turn to my brother's prone form nearby. "Unconscious, but alive."

Despite his pain, relief momentarily registers on his pale features. "You and Gerold have been my greatest joy in this life," he barely manages. "I love you both so much."

"I love you too, Father." A broken sob escapes me. "Please, do not die."

His breath comes in short, clipped pants as blood pools beneath his body. His gaze grows unfocused, lifting to the sky. His grasp on my hand weakens with each passing moment.

"You must save the city, Halla," he whispers. "Promise me."

"I will, Father. I will."

His head drops, and he closes his eyes. His hand slips from mine and falls to the ground beside him. Pain and devastation fill me. I lift his head into my lap and raise my voice in anguish to the sky.

Healer Althea rushes toward me. Her normally tightly woven silver hair loose from her braid and covered in flakes of gray ash. Her worried gaze darts to my father's still form then back to me. "Princess!"

Drawing in a deep breath, I blink back my tears and steel myself. "Take care of my brother, Althea."

"Halla!" Her gaze drops to the bloodied sword in my hand. "What are you going to do?"

I grip the sword tightly as I turn my gaze toward the city. "I'm going to slay the dragon."

CHAPTER 2

HALLA

With one final glance at my father's body, I force myself to push down my fear. I made him a promise, and now, I will keep it. If I do not slay the dragon, everyone will die. He will not stop until Solwyck is reduced to rubble and ash.

I turn to the edge of the castle rooftop, scanning the city in search of the monster.

People rush through the streets below, racing downhill to the sea. The only place fire cannot touch, where they believe they'll be safe.

I watch ships set off from the harbor, full of our citizens. My eyes widen in horror when the dragon heads toward them, releasing a torrent of flame across the decks.

Rage twists deep inside me. Sword in hand, I step onto the ledge. My heart thunders in my chest as he makes a wide arc back through the city, raining down fire and destruction as he approaches the castle. I draw in a deep and steadying breath, preparing myself to attack.

If I time it right, I can impale him. If I miss, I will fall to my death.

The heavy flapping of his wings creates swirling patterns through the thick smoke rising from the fires below. Time slows, and the space between each beat of my pulse spreads across an eternity as he flies toward me in a blur of golden scales.

Fear tightens my chest, but I force myself to focus and speak aloud to steel my courage. “I am Princess Halla of Solwyck. I tremble before no one and nothing. I am proud, unbent and unbroken. And today, I will avenge my father and save my people and my kingdom.”

The world shifts into slow motion as the dragon draws closer. His golden scales shimmering iridescent in the last of the sun’s rays. By the time it has set, I will most likely be dead. But if my death can save my people and my kingdom, it will be a sacrifice well made.

The golden eye of the dragon locks onto mine a moment before he opens his mouth, releasing a torrent of fire and destruction upon the castle as he passes beneath me. With my sword gripped firmly in both hands, I angle it down and jump. My heart hammers and time slows as I fall through ash and smoke.

My father’s sword has seen many battles and defended our family and our kingdom for several generations. As my blade finds its mark and sinks deep into the dragon’s scaled flesh, I can feel the spirits of my ancestors gathering around me, readying to welcome me home.

The dragon releases a bellowing roar, twisting and writhing beneath me.

I cling to my sword as the wind pulls at my form, trying to rip me from his back. I cannot let go or I’ll most assuredly fall to my death.

He turns his head and releases a stream of fire. The

flames sear my armor, heating the metal and burning my skin. A pained cry escapes me as I grasp the metal, scalding my palm, and rip the armor from my chest as he begins a spiraling descent toward the sea.

His wings billow like great sails for a moment before he folds them to his back and dives to the ocean. The water rushes beneath us with dizzying speed, and I can do nothing but hold on and brace myself for the impact.

CHAPTER 3

ERRIK

I swim beside my brother, hugging the shoreline. We watch, horrified, as the golden dragon sets fire to the city of Solwyck. Alarms blare through the streets as people cry out in terror, fleeing toward the only place they believe is safe—the sea.

Ships hastily push off from the harbor, filled with women and children trying to escape the destructive power of the dragon. He flies over the boats, releasing a stream of fire that sets the decks aflame.

Several other vessels try to take off, and our people swim out beside them, beckoning humans into the water for their safety. Some flee their ships and jump into the sea.

"Save as many as you can!" I yell, directing our people to help any of the humans who cannot swim to stay afloat.

But there are far more humans than Mer here. Most of my kind take to the deeper waters and stay there, preferring to avoid the land dwellers as much as they can. I watch in despair as a woman and her two children remain on the deck of one of the burning ships, refusing to retreat into the water.

I call out to her, "We will catch you and your children. We will help you to swim."

Her eyes are full of fear, but she staunchly refuses to listen. "No. You will drown us."

That these humans still believe a ridiculous myth spread to explain fishermen who are lost at sea confounds me. "You will drown anyway if you remain where you are."

Instead of listening to reason, she takes her two children and runs below deck. I cannot bear to consider their fate, burning alive when they could be safe.

Rappelling up one side and gripping the edge of the deck, I pull myself onto the burning ship.

"Errik!" My brother cries. "What are you doing?"

"Trying to save them."

"No! You'll burn with the ship if you go below deck!"

"I have to try!"

It is cumbersome to move above water with only two arms and a tail, especially when one has lived one's life completely underwater in a weightless environment. Heat sears my skin and my scales as I drag myself across the deck to the hold.

The door is sealed shut, so I pound on the outside. "Come out! Let us help you!"

When I hear no answer, I brace myself then slam my shoulder against the door repeatedly until it flies inward, shattering against the cabin walls.

Thick smoke billows from the hold. I cough when it invades my lungs, clogging until I can barely breathe.

"You must come out! You'll die in here."

No one answers, and I do not know if they are already dead, but I cannot leave without trying.

"Errik!" My brother's voice sounds beside me, startling me.

"Toren, what are you doing here?"

"I've come to help you."

I don't want to risk my younger brother's safety, but we don't have much time. I start down the stairs, my tail dragging awkwardly behind me. When I reach the bottom, I notice the woman and her children are not alone. Another woman and young girl lie unconscious beside them.

Without hesitation, Toren and I begin hauling their limp forms back up the stairs. I'm relieved when two more of my kin appear at the door. They take the humans and send them down a chain of Mer, over the deck and to the sea, into the waiting arms of more of my people.

Once everyone is rescued, we jump back into the water. One of the children wakes with a scream. I rush to her side.

Her brown eyes are wide as she turns to me. "It is all right, little one. You are safe."

"Are you going to drown me?" she mumbles.

"No. We are going to help you to swim and keep you safe from the dragon."

She smiles tremulously.

An anguished wail echoes from the city, and I whip my head in that direction to spot a woman crouched atop Solwyck castle, leaning over a body.

"Look!" one of the humans cries out, pointing to her. "It's Princess Halla!"

I watch as she stands, sword in hand. The wind catches her long, scarlet hair as she strides to the edge of the rooftop.

"She's going to jump!" someone yells. "No! Not our princess!"

Dressed from head to toe in armor, she stands on the ledge with her sword upraised as if readying for battle.

The dragon flies toward her, and I watch in stunned

silence as she jumps from the edge and impales his back, sinking her sword deep into the flesh between his wings.

The city shakes with his roar, and he begins twisting and turning, trying to shake her. She grips the sword handle, stubbornly refusing to let go.

The dragon begins a spiraling descent toward the sea. He twists again and crashes into the water.

My heart stops when the princess is thrown from his back. She slams against a nearby rock formation, her body releasing an audible *crack* as she makes impact with the unforgiving stone. I swim toward her, my tail beating frantically through the water; desperate to save her.

A rushing wave approaches behind the princess, and I know I will not reach her in time. Accelerating as best I can, I watch the turbulent sea toss her limp form from the rock and force her beneath the surface. Panic tightens my chest when I dive below the water and see her tumbling under the rolling wave.

She is still and unmoving when I wrap my arms around her back. I spin her to face me, and her eyes snap open. *"Princess Halla."* I reach for her with my mind. *"You must stay awake."*

Flame-red hair frames her face, and blue eyes search mine. She reaches out and brushes her fingers across my cheek.

"Your eyes... they are glowing. Are you an angel? Will you send me to join my father in the great halls of my ancestors?" she replies in my mind.

My heart clenches. *"No, but I am going to save you."*

Without hesitation, I grip the back of her head, threading my fingers through her long, red hair. I pull her into an embrace and seal my mouth over hers, giving her my kiss so that she may breathe underwater.

When I pull back, I am relieved to see her breathing.

Though all Mer possess this ability, I have never used it to save a human before. *"My first,"* she thinks aloud, struggling to stay conscious. *"My first kiss."*

She closes her eyes and goes still. Fear steals through me that she is dead. Only the rise and fall of her chest tell me she still lives. I must get her to help. She needs a Healer.

I make my way to the rocky shoreline beneath the castle walls. In the distance, I notice several Mer helping the humans back to the beach. Now that the dragon has been slain, it is safe for them to return to their city, but their work has only just begun.

The air is thick with smoke. Ash falls like snow, blanketing the buildings and streets. The once shining and proud city of Solwyck, known as the jewel of the kingdom, is on fire and burning.

Halla's form is limp in my arms as I pull her onto the obsidian sand beneath the dark cliff wall of the castle. A glance at my surroundings reveals that no one is coming this way. All are swimming toward the main beach and the harbor.

I lift my gaze to the palace overhead and notice a woman with long silver hair staring down at me from the rooftops. "Princess!" she shrieks and disappears behind the wall.

Halla stirs beside me. I reach down and take her hand. "Princess Halla. Please hold on. Help is coming."

I've never seen a human up close before. Her long, red hair fans beneath her like a beautiful halo against the obsidian sand. I trace my eyes over her face, noting the fine and delicate structure of her nose, brows, and cheeks. The tops of her ears are rounded instead of sharp-tipped like mine. Gently, I cup her cheek and brush the pad of my thumb across her petal-soft skin. She is the most beautiful female my eyes have ever beheld.

Her eyelids flutter open, revealing eyes as blue and deep

as the sea. Sunlight breaks through the clouds, accentuating the many spots on her otherwise pale skin. "What happened?" she murmurs.

Gently, I brush the hair back from her face. "You killed the dragon. You saved the city of Solwyck, Princess Halla."

She shifts slightly in my arms, hissing in pain at the movement. "Everything hurts. Am I dying?"

Her words strike terror in my heart. "No. Help is coming. You must hold on."

The tide rushes over us, and as the water retreats, I note the fine trail of red that follows in its wake.

Frantically, I move my hands down her form. Her tunic and pants are tattered and scorched by the fire, revealing the pale expanse of flesh beneath, interspersed with areas of redness and blistering skin. I reach beneath her, tracing my fingers across her back to search for the injury that is bleeding. When I pull my hand away, it is covered with blood.

I rip a long strip of fabric from her tunic and wrap it tightly around her torso, desperate to staunch the bleeding as I shoot another glance at the castle and cry out. "Help! The Princess is injured! She needs a Healer!"

"I'm coming!" I recognize the woman's voice somewhere nearby. Close, but not close enough, I fear.

A featherlight touch on my cheek draws my attention back to Halla. Her blue eyes are bright with tears as she brushes the tips of her fingers over my face. "Are you an angel?"

Despite my worry, a faint smile crests my lips. She has already asked me this before. I take her hand in mine. "No."

"Then why do I feel like I'm dying?" she breathes as another tear slips down her cheek.

I brush it away with the pad of my thumb. "You must live, Princess Halla," I whisper. "You must live."

Her head falls back, and fear wraps tight around my chest as she falls unconscious.

The sound of footsteps crunching over the rocky sand behind me draws my attention. I turn just as the woman from earlier comes into view. Her long silver hair is tied in a loose knot at the nape of her neck and her face is pale and drawn as she drops to her knees beside the princess.

"She's bleeding," I tell her. "She needs help."

"I'll tend to her."

The sound of shouting voices carries on the wind and the Healer's eyes go wide. "You should go. Some still believe the terrible lies about your people trying to drown them."

"But—"

"Thank you for saving her, but you must go before anyone else comes."

I dip my chin in a firm nod and retreat into the water. I swim out to a nearby rock and hide behind it, watching as the woman gathers the princess in her arms. Two guards rush to aid her and carry the princess back into the castle.

Please. I send a silent prayer to any gods who may be listening. *Save her.*

CHAPTER 4

HALLA

Strange images rush toward me, and I wake with a start. Even as my eyes blink open, I still see him—the man who saved me. His eyes are as blue as the northern sea, his hair is the color of the obsidian stone cliffs along the shoreline, and he observes me with a strange mixture of sadness and concern.

Closing my eyes, I can still feel the whisper of his touch across my face as he spoke to me in the ancient tongue. *You must live, Princess Halla. You must live.*

"Halla?" A familiar voice calls from the hallway.

"Enter!" I respond.

My brother, Gerold, enters a moment later with Healer Althea. His warm, blue eyes, so like mine, travel over me as he sits on the edge of the bed and takes my hand. "Good morning, my dear sister. How are you feeling?"

"Fine," I lie, and his expression falls. It's been a little over a month since the dragon's attack on our city. Gerold and I have always been close, and he can tell when I do not speak the truth. I want so badly to tell him exactly how I'm feeling, but the golden crown atop his head, nestled in his red hair, reminds me of all the burdens now resting on his shoulders. I do not want to add to them.

"You know you can tell me anything," he offers. "I may be king now, but I am still your brother, and I will always have time for you."

A faint smile ghosts my lips. "Sometimes I think it's as if you can read my mind."

Althea tenderly brushes the hair back from my brow. "Your late mother always commented that you not only looked like twins but thought the same way, too."

Gerold's smile doesn't erase the sadness in his eyes. He misses her just as much as I do. Now that Father is gone as well, the pain cuts even deeper.

"Can you move your feet for me?" Althea asks.

Clenching my jaw, I turn my focus to my legs, willing them to move. I still have not regained full use of my lower body. At least some of the feeling has returned, but that doesn't help me to walk.

Slowly, I flex and extend my foot. She places her palm against the sole and asks me to push against her resistance.

My brother observes intently as I grit my teeth and struggle to push against her hand, but my lower body is still so weak, it's disheartening.

Althea does her best to remain cheery as she lifts her gray head. "You are improving."

What she doesn't say is that I have not improved much.

I squeeze Gerold's hand. "Have the Fae agreed to send their Healer?"

I'm anxious to know if he's heard anything. Healers from many kingdoms have come at his request to see if they can do any more than Althea, but so far, no one has been able to help me.

Gerold sent an ambassador to the kingdom of Anara, hoping they might send one of their Healers to assess me. We never would have asked them for anything before, since it was clear they had no love for humans. But Gerold took a chance to send someone anyway, asking for help. The Fae are my last hope.

Well, technically not my last. There is always the blood witch who lives just outside the city. I shudder inwardly at the thought. Witches are dangerous, and deals with them should never be made lightly, for there is always a steep cost.

"Did you sleep well?" Gerold asks, and I know he's really asking if the nightmares of the day I was injured have finally stopped. They haven't, but instead of telling him this, I focus on the part of the dream that intrigues me the most.

"I dreamed of him again. Have you found out anything?"

He lowers his gaze. Ever since I told him of the man who saved me, he has searched high and low, but no one has stepped forward. I want to thank him, but it's more than that. I want to know the face that haunts my dreams every night and fills my thoughts as I go through my days.

"Do you remember anything else that might help us to identify him?"

A new part of the dream came to me last night—something I did not recall until now. I reach up to touch my mouth, remembering the brush of his lips upon mine. "I think he was one of the Mer, Gerold."

Gerold cocks his head to the side. "Why do you say that?"

My face heats in embarrassment. As close as I am to my brother, I do not want to tell him about the kiss. I shrug. "Just a feeling."

"Do you remember a tail? That might be a clue," Gerold grins teasingly. "Unless..." He arches a brow. "It is as I've suspected, and he was a conjuring of your imagination."

I purse my lips. "I did not imagine him."

"It's not unusual to hallucinate when you've been heavily injured. The mind can play tricks and create false images." At my disapproving look, he shrugs. "Maybe you *were* saved by one of the Mer, but he was long gone by the time we found you on the shore." He turns to Althea. "Althea found you, and she saw no one nearby, is that not right?"

Althea nods. "You were alone on the beach, Halla."

I've heard this all before, but in my heart, I know I was not alone. I feel it. "I need to find him, Gerold. I want to thank him."

He sighs. "If he was one of the Mer, you know how they are—an elusive lot. They do not like to interact with our kind." A grin tilts his lips. "He did not steal your heart away, now did he?"

Heat blooms across my cheeks as the memory of the kiss overtakes my thoughts once again. "No," I reply. "I merely wish to thank the man who saved my life. That is all."

Gerold arches a teasing brow. "Well, if he was a Merman and he returns for you... If at any time you hear a siren's call and feel compelled to go to the sea, please inform one of the guards before you do so, all right?"

I playfully hit his arm, and he starts laughing.

"Don't worry," I tell him. "It's not as if I could make my way down to the water alone anyway."

Laughter dies in my throat as I look at the wheeled chair by the bed. It was a wonderful idea, but not much use here in Solwyck. The city is built upon a hill that slopes toward the sea across many stairs and steep inclines. I cannot simply wheel down without help.

Gerold's expression turns grim. "I am sorry, my dear sister. Our men are working as fast as they can to accommodate your chair."

His crew of workers is constructing inclines for my chair so that I may move about the castle more easily, but until then, the only place I can be semi-independent is on this level of the castle. If I want to go from one level to the next, I must ask the aid of the guards or my brother to carry me where I wish to go. It is frustrating. Especially since I've always taken pride in my independence.

I clench my jaw, trying but failing to keep the bitter edge from my tone as I reply, "I only wish you did not have to make any changes to accommodate that infernal chair."

"Do not sulk," Althea gently chastises. "It is not becoming of a princess."

Her words make me feel as if I'm seven years old again. Althea may be a Healer, but she has also been like a surrogate mother to Gerold and me ever since our mother died.

"I'm not sulking." *I'm devastated. There's a difference.*

Althea turns to Gerold, who stands and walks to the balcony to give us some privacy as she lifts my dress. I follow her gaze as she inspects my ruined flesh. I remind myself that it would have been worse if I hadn't been wearing armor when I was hit by the dragon's fire. The thick scar tissue covers much of my torso, and I tense when her fingers trace over the uneven areas on my skin.

She cups my cheek. "It could have been worse, Halla. At least your face was spared, my angel," she says, using the beloved nickname she bestowed upon me as a child.

Tears sting my eyes, but I blink them back. "Who will want me like this?" I gesture to my burned flesh and my legs.

Only a few days ago King Gronlund of Skallog sent word that, due to my condition, he was dissolving the betrothal agreement between me and his son, Prince Edwyrd. I wasn't in love with Edwyrd, but the rejection hurt just the same.

Gently, Althea combs the hair back from my face. "Any man who cannot see past the outside to the beautiful, brave person you are within would not be worthy of you."

I nod. She is right; perhaps I am blessed in a way. I might

have married a man only to find out later that he wanted me only for my title. This way, if I do find someone, I'll know that he loves me for me.

I grab my legs and drag them over the edge of the bed. I pull my wheeled chair close and use my board to transfer.

"I'll be ready in a moment," I tell Althea and my brother as I make my way to the cleansing room.

It doesn't take me as long to get dressed as in the first days after the accident. I'm both glad and disheartened at how quickly I've acclimated to living without the full use of my legs.

Gerold carries me downstairs to the dining hall for our first meal. One of the staff follows with my chair. The guards bow as we pass, and when they straighten, I see the burning devotion that has become all too commonplace since I awoke after I killed the dragon. I'm a hero to the kingdom and its citizens.

Sighing heavily, I glance down at my now useless legs, thinking of all I lost to achieve this title and the love of my people.

I struggle to remain cheerful as we gather around the table.

"We are making great strides in cleaning the city. We are even beginning to rebuild. I can arrange for you to take a tour, if you'd like," Gerold offers.

The last thing I want is to be carted around in a carriage, looking down on hardworking people as if I'm some pampered princess. "Thank you, but I'd prefer to stay here for now."

A man approaches the table, bowing low before me and my brother. "Your Grace," he begins. "We've finished the ramp as you instructed. Would you like to inspect the work?"

Gerold smiles. "Excellent news. We would love to." He stands. "Come, Halla. I believe this will brighten your day."

I don't tell him that it will take much more than a ramp to make me happy. Instead, I follow him in my wheeled chair, curious to see what he's had done.

I'm surprised when he leads me outside the castle into the side courtyard and the passage that leads down to the sea. I roll to a stop, waiting for Gerold to turn around and lift me into his arms since we're approaching more stairs.

He turns back to me, a sly grin quirking his lips. "Are you coming or not?"

My brow furrows as I wheel past him. My face splits in a bright smile when I spot the newly constructed ramp that leads down to the shoreline. I've always loved the sea, and Gerold knows I would often jog back and forth along the beach and then go for a swim after my run. Carefully, I guide my chair down the ramp as Gerold follows me.

When I reach the shoreline, I notice flat stones laid in the sand, creating a path I can roll my chair down.

Gerold grins. "What do you think?"

"I love it!" I beam.

I do. This is the best present he could have possibly given me.

I turn my gaze out to the sea and my jaw drops when I notice a blue fin sink beneath the surface. A flash of memory flits through my mind. I remember a blue tail when I was floating, limp and broken, in the water.

I scan the area, watching for any movement or sign of a Mer.

"What are you doing?" Gerold asks.

"I… thought I saw something."

"Your Merman rescuer?" A teasing smile crests his lips. "Perhaps he's come to steal you away."

I would roll my eyes, but I'm too busy staring at the water. I wish to find him—this mysterious Merman who rescued me. He haunts my dreams, and I need to know why.

CHAPTER 5

ERRIK

It's been a little over a month and I've heard no word about Princess Halla. I cannot stop thinking about her, wondering if she is all right. Against my father's wishes, I have been swimming along the shoreline, hoping to discover whether she still lives.

However, the docks are quieter than normal. Most of the ships were burned and now lie at the bottom of the sea after the dragon's attack. The people of Solwyck are busy cleaning up, trying to rebuild their once glorious city.

Sailors and dockworkers are usually a rather chatty lot, but it seems even they have little news of her condition. There are rumors that she will never walk again. I pray this isn't true.

Walking for humans is like swimming for my kind. I cannot imagine how difficult my life would be if I suddenly lost the ability to swim.

Movement in the water beside me startles me. I spin toward it and find my brother, Toren.

"I knew I'd find you here," he says. "Why have you returned? Father will be angry if he finds out where you are."

I arch a brow. "Then I suggest you do not tell him."

He purses his lips. "Father was already angry at you for turning down the offer of betrothal to Princess Allana. Imagine if he found out now that you're here after he has expressly told us to avoid humans."

"And who will tell him?" I cross my arms over my chest. "You are the only one who knows."

He runs his fingers roughly through his short, dark hair. "I will not report you, but if anyone else sees you out here, word is bound to get back to him. Why are you still coming here? What are you hoping to find?"

I try to think of a lie but finally decide I do not want to keep secrets from my brother. We have always been honest with each other, and I don't want to end that now.

"The woman I saved—she was Princess Halla. I merely wish to know if she still lives."

"Is that all?" he asks, a hint of sarcasm in his voice.

My brother knows me too well. "That's all," I reply, but he doesn't seem convinced.

He studies me with narrowed eyes. "Well, you shouldn't be here. You need to come home. Father was looking for you; that's why I came. To warn you."

Frustration burns through me. "I will return shortly. For now, I—"

I stop short when something catches my attention out of the corner of my eye. I whip my head toward the castle and notice a flash of red hair. I recognize the princess. A tall man with hair of the same color walks alongside her as she rolls down the path in a strange, wheeled chair.

It reminds me of the carriages the humans sometimes ride around in, but those are always pulled by horses. I dive beneath the water and swim closer, hoping to get a better look.

When I surface, I conceal myself behind a large rock formation jutting above the water line. Toren follows me.

"What are you doing?" His voice is a low hiss. "They might see us."

"That's the princess. I want to see how she is doing. Besides, the land dwellers know there are Mer in these waters. We helped them during the attack, remember? What does it matter if they see us?"

"That was an exception. Humans are dangerous, and many of them believe we are, too. Do you not remember the family we forcibly had to save because they'd rather risk their lives in a burning ship than accept our aid?"

I frown. "Not all humans dislike us."

"Then why are we hiding?" He huffs, gesturing toward the beach. "We're practically spying on the princess now. Why is that, Errik?"

I clench my jaw. "We're hiding because she is with a male. We do not want him to believe we are a threat. You've seen how protective they are of their females. It's almost as if they believe we mean to steal them away."

Toren laughs, then his expression grows curious. "I wonder if that really works?"

"What?"

"Our song," he replies. "Does it really lure the humans to the sea?"

I shrug. "I think it is mere curiosity that draws them to us when we sing. Not some sort of bewitching enchantment."

It's terrible that this rumor makes humans so wary of us. I think back on the woman who would have rather died on a ship with her children than trust us. Even after she regained consciousness and realized we had saved them, she fought our people as they tried to help her back to shore. Fear often breeds hatred, to all our detriment.

Long ago, our kind were enemies, but we finally made a truce with the land dwellers. The last thing we need is renewed hostility between us. So, I struggle to believe that some humans are still fearful, even after we helped them during the dragon's attack.

Toren and I continue to observe Princess Halla and the man walking behind her as they move along the shoreline beneath the castle. The black cliff wall gleams with a pearlescent sheen beneath the rays of the sun.

The castle is made of shimmering, white stone, and sits atop the cliff wall. The spiraling towers stand proudly beneath the pale blue sky. The shimmering silver rooftops are like glowing beacons. The bold, blue-and-silver banner of Solwyck castle hangs from the tallest tower, fluttering in the wind.

This part of the coast is more rock than sand. I observe as the princess struggles to move the chair. It would undoubtedly be easier for her to walk, and I fear the rumors must be true. She has lost the use of her legs.

They stop, and the man takes her hand. He brings the back of it to his lips in a brief kiss, then leaves, walking back along the shore until he turns and makes his way up the winding path to the castle.

The warm, saline breeze whips through her long red hair as her luminous blue eyes watch the sea. The tide is low now, so there is no worry of her being overcome by waves, but I wonder what she means to do down here.

Cautiously, I slip beneath the water and move closer, concealing myself behind another grouping of rocks jutting up from the water. Toren follows, and even though I am not facing him, I can sense his judgment, heavy at my back.

When I stop, he moves up beside me. "Grandfather once

told me that the castle was built on that cliff because of these rocks."

"What do you mean?"

He glances around at the many tight formations that line this part of the shallows. "Not only is it shallow here, but the rocks make an approach difficult to navigate. So, there is little chance an invading force could attack the castle directly by sea." I had never considered this, but he is right. "Father says there is a good chance another kingdom, or even pirates, may try to invade."

Alarm skitters across my skin. "Why?"

He gestures to the ruined city. "They have been weakened by the dragon's attack."

Worry tightens my chest as I turn my gaze back to Halla. "Surely, Father would provide them aid if they were attacked by sea."

"I do not think so," Toren replies. "You know how much he hates them after Mother's death."

"Mother's death was an accident."

"It does not matter. He holds them and their ships responsible."

I recall that horrible day. Our people were trying to save the humans during a terrible storm. They were caught out on the open sea. Their ships broke apart beneath a strong wave, injuring and killing several of our kin who were trying to help. Mother was among them.

Pushing the dark memory from my mind, I return my attention to Princess Halla.

My jaw drops when she gathers the hem of her tunic and lifts it over her head, discarding the fabric onto the sand beside her. She then unfastens her pants, carefully tilting her body on the chair as she slides the material down her legs.

"What is she doing?" Toren asks beside me. "I thought the humans disliked nudity."

He's right. While our people think nothing of it, the humans only disrobe to bathe or to mate. The only reason our females wear shells to hide their breasts is that they hate the attention they receive from human males otherwise when they swim too close to shore.

I notice that Halla still wears a band of material across her chest to cover her breasts and a scrap of fabric between her legs that hides her pelvis. For some reason, the sight of her makes my heart rate quicken.

"I do not know," I reply to my brother as I continue to watch her, wondering what she plans to do.

She grips the handrails of her chair tightly and pushes herself up as if trying to stand. I frown when her arms tremble with the exertion of holding her weight while her legs do not move to support her. She collapses onto the rock and sand.

I gasp. Without thinking, I rush toward her, my tail propelling me at full speed beneath the water to reach her quickly.

"Where are you going?" Toren shouts.

"To help," I call over my shoulder, not bothering to look back.

"Stop, Errik. You should not—"

I dive beneath the water, unwilling to hear the rest of his sentence. I know what I'm doing is wrong, but I cannot leave her lying on the beach. I want to at least help her back into her chair.

"Errik!" My brother's voice rings in my head beneath the water as he uses our mind link to speak to me. *"Come back!"*

"No!"

Ahead, I stop short when I notice Princess Halla has entered the water. Her legs float behind her, unmoving as she raises her arms in long strokes and begins swimming out to sea.

My eyes widen as I notice the heavy scarring across her torso from the dragon's flame. I cannot imagine how painful that must have been for her.

"What is she doing?"

"I do not know," Toren replies. *"But it is none of our concern. You need to come back with me. Now."*

"I will come later."

"Fine, but do not say I didn't warn you. If Father catches you out here, you will be punished."

I don't bother to answer because he's right. Yet I do not care. I'm more interested in following Halla.

She continues swimming, keeping her head above water because humans cannot breathe beneath the waves as I do. I remain hidden beneath the surface, following behind her at a safe distance to avoid alerting her to my presence.

Exhaustion is evident in her features and movements as she begins to struggle with each stroke. Yet, she perseveres. Ahead lies one of the larger rock formations, so expansive it is like a small island. Rocks surround and shield its beach from the view of the castle. I suspect this destination is her goal.

Sure enough, when she reaches the island, she pulls herself onto the rock. Panting heavily, she drags her legs out of the water and twists onto her back, staring up at the sky. I hoist myself onto a rock behind her so that I might observe her while remaining hidden. I do not wish to scare her.

The thin bands of fabric, that cover her, cling to her body. The outline of her breasts peek through the silken material, as well as a curious patch of red hair between her legs, which are not entirely still. I watch her slowly move her feet, but when she sits up and lifts her thighs with her hands to position them, I grow concerned.

It seems the rumors are true. She has very minimal use of her lower half.

I observe as she props herself up against a rock, staring out at the waves. She lowers her head into her hands, and I notice the slight quake of her shoulders. When a hoarse sob escapes her, I realize that she is crying.

Her sadness tears at my heart. "Are you all right?" I ask from my hiding place.

She stills and wipes at her face. "Who's there?"

"I mean you no harm, Princess," I offer quickly to soothe her fears.

She turns her head, searching for me. "Your voice," she says. "I know it. Who are you?"

Does she remember me? Before I can ask, she speaks again.

"You're the one who saved me, aren't you?"

"Yes."

"What is your name?"

I hesitate for a moment, uncertain if I should identify myself. Instead, I ask her a question. "Why do you cry?"

She wipes at her face again, brushing away tears. "Because I cannot use my legs. My back was injured when I fell from the dragon's back and crashed into the sea." Her voice catches. "The Healers do not know if I will ever be able to walk again."

Sadness plagues me. A human without the use of their legs is like a Mer unable to use their tail to swim. "I am sorry, Princess. Truly."

She sniffs and wipes again at her tears. "I've searched for you."

"You have?"

She nods. "I do not recall much, but I do remember that if you had not rescued me, I would have drowned. I wanted to thank you for rescuing me."

"You are welcome, Princess."

"Halla," she says. "You can call me Halla."

"Halla," I repeat her name aloud.

"Are you one of the Mer?"

I hesitate before answering, "Yes."

"Can I see you?"

I still. "Are you certain you wish this?"

She nods.

"You are not afraid?" I ask, just to be sure.

"Why would I be? You rescued me." She pauses. "If you will not come out, can you at least give me your name so I might thank you properly for saving my life?"

"My name is Errik."

"Errik," she repeats, and I love how my name sounds on her tongue… more than I know I should. "Thank you, Errik. I am forever in your debt."

"You owe me nothing, Halla. I am glad I was able to rescue you."

She lowers her gaze to the sand. "Will you at least tell me if your eyes are blue like I remember? I see them almost every night in my dreams, you know."

My heart stutters in my chest. "You dream of me?"

A huff of air leaves her parted lips as she smiles. "Yes."

I draw in a deep, steeling breath and emerge from my hiding place. As I do, the thought occurs to me that she may not like what she sees. After all, I am very different from her kind. I may not spend much time around humans, but I've heard enough from my kin to know that they do not easily accept those who are different.

Some even find us monstrous to behold.

As soon as she turns to face me, I'm struck by her beauty. She is more stunning than I remember. Her eyes are as blue as the ocean. Her red hair falls over her shoulders in long, silken waves. My gaze travels down her form to the sensuous curve of her breasts and the gentle flare of her hips. For all the strength I witnessed in her the day she slew the dragon,

I'm surprised by how slight and delicate she appears. The women of my kind possess heavily muscled forms.

Worry fills me when I notice her mouth drifting open and a strange red coloring flaring across the bridge of her nose and cheeks, accentuating the many spots across her otherwise pale skin.

My heart sinks, for I fear she finds me hideous to behold.

"Your eyes," she breathes, her voice full of wonder. "They are glowing. Just as I remembered." Her expression changes and she tips her head to the side. "Why did you leave?"

Her question confuses me. "Leave?"

"My brother said when they found me, you were already gone."

"Forgive me. Hiding is a habit, I'm afraid. Humans have not always been friendly to my kind, so we are taught from infancy never to be caught on land."

"Oh." She lowers her gaze, and her small brow furrows. "Why are you here, then? Why did you follow me?"

"I..." I try to think of an excuse to skirt the truth but can invent none, so I decide to be honest. "I have worried for you ever since that day. I wanted to make sure you were all right."

"Aside from my legs, I am fine." Her blue eyes brighten with tears. She sniffs and brushes the drops from her cheeks with her hands. "Really, I shouldn't be crying. It's not as if there is no hope. My brother has sent for a Fae Healer who has agreed to try and help me. They are known for their healing prowess." She pauses and looks down at her feet, slowly curling her toes. "And I have some movement and feeling, which is better than none."

Happiness blooms in my chest. "This is good."

"Yes," she agrees. "It gives me hope."

CHAPTER 6

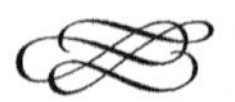

HALLA

He is the most gorgeous man I have ever seen. He has short, straight, black hair that hangs just above his brow. The tops of his ears are pointed like the Fae. With a sharp jaw that could cut glass, his face is regal, but his eyes draw me in most.

Their blue glow reminds me of the sea alight with a sunset. I allow my gaze to travel down his form. His body is powerful, built of lean, sculpted muscle. His upper body appears mostly human before the tan flesh-colored scales slowly turn into a deep blue tail, starting at his waist, that matches the ocean. It is longer than I expected, and the wide fan on the end is nothing short of stunning, swiping lazily back and forth before him.

His scales shimmer beneath the sunlight, and I note that his entire body seems to glisten with a pearlescent sheen. His fingers are tipped with lethal black claws, but they do not scare me. If he'd wanted to hurt me, he could have done so while he was following me earlier. When he smiles, he bares two rows of gleaming, white fangs. Instead of making me feel afraid, they only add a lethal edge to his handsomeness.

I lift my gaze back to his glowing blue eyes, and the contact makes my heart flutter. *Can he tell that I find him attractive?*

He lowers his gaze. "Forgive me. I do not wish to scare you."

"Scare me?"

He blinks. "You are not afraid?"

I smile. "Why would I fear you?"

"My appearance does not bother you?"

"No," I deny vehemently. "You are the most beautiful man I've ever seen." Heat sears my face and neck, and I wince inwardly as the words escape my lips before I even realize I've spoken them aloud.

He arches a teasing brow. "I believe the word you were searching for is *handsome.*"

"Yes, of course, it is," I laugh softly, both surprised and glad by his teasing, avoiding any awkwardness between us after my words about his appearance.

His lips curve in a gorgeous smile that makes my heart rate quicken.

He shifts slightly, drawing my attention back to his tail, and I grow concerned. "How long can you remain out of the water?"

"I am fine for now. My people often lie in the sun for many hours at a time without any consequences."

My shoulder sag in relief. Cautiously, I scoot closer to him. "May I touch you?"

He stills. His piercing blue eyes study me for a moment before he nods.

Carefully, I reach out and touch his face. I brush my fingers across his cheek, marveling at the silken texture of his scales. "Your scales are so smooth," I whisper more to myself than to him.

"Is that bad?" he asks.

"No. Just… different than I expected. May I touch your tail?"

He grins and lifts his tail toward me. Carefully, I trace the tips of my fingers over his scales and find that they feel much like the rest of him. When I trace my fingers toward his tail fin, he carefully lays it on my lap. The membrane is not as delicate as it appears; it is thick and tough like cartilage.

"Halla?" A voice calls from the shoreline, and I recognize my brother. "Halla!"

I whip my head in the direction of the beach. "I'm all right!" I shout. "I'll swim back to you!" I turn to Errik. "It's my brother, Gerold. I have to go."

I start to pull myself back to the water, but Errik calls out. "Wait!"

I look back at him curiously. "What is it?"

"Will I see you again?"

I hesitate. "You… wish to see me again?"

A devastatingly handsome smile curves his lips. "Yes."

I cannot help but smile in return. "All right."

"Will you meet me here tomorrow?"

I nod.

"Tomorrow then," he confirms. Without another word, he slips beneath the water and swims away.

CHAPTER 7

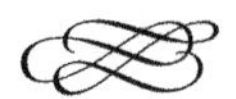

ERRIK

She was not afraid of me, and she agreed to meet me tomorrow. I cannot deny that this pleases me greatly, for I wish to spend more time with her. I follow under the water to make sure she reaches the shore safely. Though she is strong, there are creatures in the ocean that are dangerous even to my kind.

As soon as she drags herself onto the beach, I swim back out to the rock, concealing myself as I observe her.

I now know that the tall man I saw with her earlier is her brother, Gerold. I've heard much about him. He is strong in his own right. In the days following the attack, I witnessed him organizing his people to begin cleaning and rebuilding the city.

As soon as they disappear around the rocks toward their castle, I head back home. The sun is already low on the water, and I'm sure Father is wondering where I've been.

I must conjure a good excuse before I arrive. If I must

make one up on the spot, he'll easily detect the lie. Father has always been skilled at reading people.

As I make my way back to the city, images of Halla flash through my mind. Her eyes are even bluer than the sea and her hair is the color of flame. A strange yet lovely contrast of fire and water.

Several of my people swim past me when I enter the city. A few of the females cast appraising glances my way, but I note that none of them are as lovely as Halla. She is the most beautiful female I have ever seen. I wish that she was Mer or that I were human. If only…

By the time I reach the castle, it is late. The golden glow of the L'sair crystals illuminates the structure, lending an ethereal appearance to the palace and the city that surrounds it.

Many kingdoms lie beneath the sea—Toren and I have accompanied Father to almost all of them—but none rival the beauty and majesty of Atena and its castle.

Tall towers of white and black pearl spiral toward the surface. They sparkle against the glowing lights like shining beacons amidst the blue water. The many surrounding buildings are made of pearl, as well, intricately carved with beautiful patterns. Groves of seaweed sway gently back and forth in the calm waters as Mer children zip between them, playing games.

As soon as I enter the palace, Toren swims to me, a grim look on his face as he speaks through the mind link. *"Father is angry. He's been searching for you all day."*

"What did you tell him?"

"Nothing. I said I could not find you."

"Why was he searching for me? He normally does not care what I do."

Toren shrugs. *"I do not know. He merely said it was important."*

"Errik!" Father's voice rings in my mind. He probably picked up on my presence through our family bond since I am nearby.

"Coming, Father," I reply dutifully.

Toren follows me toward the throne room. Sentries float on either side of the great doors. They dip their chins in salute as Toren and I enter.

Father is seated on this throne at the far end of the hall, a thunderous expression on his face. *"Where have you been?"*

"I was hunting," I lie, the best I could come up with on short notice. *"Toren says you've been searching for me most of the day. Is something wrong?"*

He narrows his eyes, most likely recognizing my lie for what it is, but he doesn't challenge my words. He swims toward me and places a hand on my shoulder. *"My son, I must speak with you about something important."*

"What is it?"

"I have found you a mate."

My head jerks back. *"A mate? Why?"*

His brows pinch together as if my question were absurd. *"You are of age—twenty-five years old—and the heir to Atena. That is why. I have negotiated a betrothal between you and Princess Luriel of the kingdom of Itlana. Your bonding will ensure peace between us, especially once you produce an heir."*

"An heir?" I ask incredulously. *"Father, you cannot be serious. You cannot possibly think I'll bond with a stranger."*

"She is a good match for you, Errik," he states firmly. *"You will bond with her to unite our kingdoms."*

"No, Father. I will not. Besides, our kingdoms are already united with a peace treaty, are they not?"

His nostrils flare as he glares at me. *"You know as well as I that treaties are not as strong as blood bondings."* I start to protest, but he waves his hand dismissively. *"Go. Do not speak anymore unless it is to tell me that you are not selfish and will put the needs of your kingdom above your own."*

His words are like a blade in my heart. I know that I have rebelled somewhat in the past, but I have never done anything serious. In truth, I have tried my best to be a worthy, dutiful son. I have only ever wanted his approval.

Dorin—Father's advisor and my mentor—purses his lips disapprovingly. *"Think on it, Errik. This betrothal would be good for you and our kingdom. Who knows? When you meet Luriel, your fate markings may appear."*

He is right. There is always a chance I could find my fated mate; perhaps it may even be Luriel. I lower my eyes to the floor. *"I will consider it, Dorin."*

CHAPTER 8

HALLA

When morning comes, I'm excited at the thought that I'll be meeting with Errik later. I dreamed of him again last night. I reach up and gently touch my lips at the memory of his mouth against mine. It was my first kiss. I know he only did it so that he could save me, but I cannot stop thinking about it.

Gerold carries me downstairs for breakfast. As we sit across from one another, he tells me about the progress that has been made on the modifications to the castle to accommodate my chair.

I listen half-heartedly, putting on my best cheery face because I know how hard he's trying to make things easier for me. But the thought of being bound to this chair forever is devastating.

As Gerold drones on, I glance at the grand staircase beyond the open double doors. We used to slide down the bannisters when we were children. Althea was always after us to stop, but we would continue anyway.

I stood at the top of those stairs in my most elegant dress and crown to greet Prince Edwyrd when he came to Solwyck seeking my hand for a betrothal. We danced most of the night in celebration after Father sealed the arrangement. I was not in love with him, but our conversation flowed well. In his eyes, I could see a man would listen to me as his partner. I'd hoped that love might come later between us, but I know now that it never will.

"Are you paying attention?" Gerold's voice pulls me back from my thoughts.

Tears sting my eyes, but I blink them back. "Of course, I am."

Sadness fills his expression. He reaches forward and takes my hand. "Halla, I do not mean to upset you. I am simply trying to make it easier for you to navigate the castle with your chair."

I pull my hand away, clenching my jaw as I study him. The pity in his eyes is more than I can bear. "You've already given up on me."

"Never," he denies. "I—"

"Yes, you have," I state firmly. "Just admit it."

He sighs heavily. "I have not given up hope that you may walk again, Halla. Why do you think I've sent for Healers from all across the land? I've even begged other kingdoms, that are not our allies, for their Healers as well. I will not give up until we've exhausted every possibility." He frowns and lowers his gaze. "Only then will I allow myself to accept it."

"Accept what?" I ask, my tone sharper than I'd intended.

He sits back in his chair and scrubs a hand across his face. "Why do you do this?"

"Do what?" I shoot back.

"Take your anger out on me."

His words pierce my heart as sure as any dagger. My anger dissipates immediately, and I reach for his hand again, squeezing it gently. "I'm sorry, Gerold. Forgive me. It's just —" my breath hitches. "Sometimes I feel so helpless, and I hate that. I hate having to rely on others so that I can get around."

"I know, my dear sister. I'm so sorry this happened to you. There is not a single day that I do not wish it were me in your stead." His eyes brighten with tears. "It should have been me, not you, Halla."

"Do not say that," I tell him. "I love you and I would never wish to trade this with you, Gerold." I pause as my gaze drops to my legs. "I would not wish it on anyone."

After breakfast, I make my way down to the shoreline. The ocean is calm today. The waves gentle and rolling instead of turbulent like they were only a few days ago. Staring out at the crystal blue sea, I breathe deep of the crisp, salted air that blows in off the water.

I've always loved the sea. I used to live for days like this. I'd run along the beach and then dive into the water to cool myself after. Althea used to tease that I was born part fish.

I cast my gaze out to one of the rock formations, far in the distance. I used to challenge myself by swimming to it. It would take every bit of my effort to make it there and then back again.

Clenching my jaw, I allow my gaze to drift over the sea. I curl my hands into fists at my side. I have never backed down from a challenge and this will not be any different. Whatever it takes, I will strengthen my body and I will walk again someday.

Carefully, I peel off my clothes, leaving me only in my undergarments. I push myself out of my chair. For a moment, I wonder if I'll be able to stand. Instead, I drop to my knees on the pebbled shoreline and drag myself into the water.

"Halla!" someone calls out, and I recognize Errik's voice right away. He swims up beside me. "Your knees are bleeding. Why did you not wait for me to help you?"

"I'm fine," I tell him.

"Does it not hurt?"

"No." I hate that it doesn't pain me when I know it should. I change the subject. "How did you know to meet me here so early?"

"I took a chance." He grins. "And I'm glad that I did."

He's so handsome, and when he smiles, my entire body flushes with warmth.

He places two fingers up under my chin, tipping my face up to his. "What does this mean?"

"What?" I ask, not sure what he's talking about.

He brushes his thumb across my cheek. "This red coloring that blooms across your skin."

My face turns even redder. "It happens when we're excited or nervous about something," I explain. "It can also happen when we're attracted to someone."

He studies me with an intense gaze. "Why do *you* turn this color now?"

"I'm excited to swim." The lie burns my tongue. "That's all."

A gorgeous grin curves his mouth. "All right. Then, let's go."

He follows beside me as I do laps back and forth between the rock formation we met at yesterday and the shore. I'm able to kick a bit with my legs, but not much. After a while, the muscles of my arms begin to burn from the exertion.

I stop and turn so that I can float on my back. Errik mimics this, floating beside me. "Why do you push yourself so much? Why not just enjoy swimming?"

I stare up at the clouds, watching the birds flying overhead. I point to them. "You see those birds?"

"Yes."

"I want to be free like that again."

He turns his gaze to me, his brow creased slightly.

I continue. "I used to feel like I could do anything. But now... I just feel so weak sometimes. I hate having to rely on others to carry me places that my chair cannot go. I just... want to be free and strong again, Errik."

"You are strong," he says.

"No, I'm not."

"Yes, you are," he counters. "I have seen Mer who have lost the use of their tails after a back injury. They still have the use of their arms, but... they give up. They refuse to swim anymore and eventually just allow themselves to fade away." His eyes meet mine. "But you do not do this. You have not given up. You are stronger than you realize, Halla."

"Not strong enough for some," I murmur, more to myself than to him.

"What do you mean?"

With a slight clench of my jaw, I cast my gaze to the sky again. "My betrothed has rejected me because of my... condition."

"Then, I say you are well rid of him," Errik states firmly.

My eyes snap to his.

"He does not deserve you."

A smile crests my lips. "Thank you, Errik."

"You do not have to thank me for speaking the truth."

I study his glowing blue eyes, noting the kindness behind them. "You are strong, Halla. Even if you do not believe it."

I hope he is right. Sometimes, I feel as if I will break from my sadness. I turn my gaze back out to the water and begin to swim more laps. I refuse to give up. Someday, I will walk again.

~

After I've done several more laps, Errik and I lay on our sides, facing each other in the sand. The small island rock formation providing privacy from the rest of the world as we gaze out at the setting sun.

The last of its golden rays casting shimmering reflections across the water's surface in a dazzling display. "I didn't realize it was already so late," I tell him.

He smiles. "Neither did I." He rolls onto his back, folding his hands behind his head. "My father's probably going to be furious when I get home. He hates when I'm out late and especially when he finds out it's near the shoreline."

"What about your mother?" I ask.

His expression falls. "She died when I was a child. She and several others were trying to help a ship that had been caught on the open sea in a storm."

I go still. "Was the ship called *The Queen's Pride?*"

"Yes, how did you—"

Tears fill my eyes. "My mother was on that ship. She died that day as well."

He reaches across and takes my hand. His palm smooth as silk as he squeezes it gently. "I am sorry for your loss, Halla."

"And I'm sorry for yours too, Errik."

He lowers his gaze. "My father hates humans now because of what happened. He blames them for her death."

"My father felt the same about Mer," I offer. "But my brother and I do not share his beliefs."

A faint smile curls Errik's mouth. "My brother and I do not share our father's either."

"You have a brother?"

"Toren. He is a few years younger than me, and not quite as handsome." He gives me a teasing grin. "Do you have more siblings?" he asks. "Or is it just you and your brother?"

"Just me and Gerold. He's a few years older than me. We've always been close." I pause. "I'm so thankful I did not lose him that day too… when the dragon attacked the city."

Still holding my hand, Errik brushes the pad of his thumb across my knuckles. "I am sorry about your father, Halla."

Emotions lodge in my throat, but I somehow manage to speak around them. "Thank you."

As his gaze holds mine, there is something about him that draws me in. It's as if my soul somehow recognizes his. I remember my mother telling me the story of how she met my father. They fell in love at first sight.

I'll admit that, when I got older, I did not believe such a thing was possible. But now that I've met Errik, I am beginning to think that I may be wrong.

There is something so familiar about him. The silence between us as we lie on the sand is neither awkward nor strained.

"Do your people believe in fate?" The question escapes my lips before I even realize I've spoken it aloud.

His glowing blue eyes study me. "Yes, we do. My parents were fated to each other."

A faint smile crests my lips. "So were mine. At least… that's what my mother always told us."

"It's strange, is it not?" he asks. "When you think of all the people who had to meet so that we could be here now."

"What do you mean?"

"All of our ancestors." A smile tilts his lips. "If they had not met, neither would we. So, in a way," he says. "Fate led us to each other, Halla."

His gaze holds mine as he reaches out and gently tucks a stray tendril of hair behind my ear. The gesture is so intimate, my cheeks flare with heat. "If I were human, what would we do, Halla?" he asks softly, and I wonder what he means.

I can interpret his words a hundred different ways, but I hope it means he feels for me as I do him.

Yet, even as I think this, I know it is impossible. He's not human and I am not Mer. No matter how much I wish I could be.

"Halla!" Gerold calls out from the shoreline. "Where are you?"

"I'm here, Gerold!" I reply. "I'm coming back!"

I turn to Errik. "I have to go. Will I see you tomorrow?"

He flashes a gorgeous smile. "Yes."

CHAPTER 9

ERRIK

I swim beneath the surface, keeping an eye on Halla as she makes her way back to shore. When she reaches it, I watch as her brother helps her back into her chair. "You should not stay in the water this late," he gently chastises. "It's cold; you might catch your death out here."

Panic stops my heart. I had no idea this could happen. I make a mental note to make certain she returns to the land far before sunset tomorrow. I do not want Halla to die.

As I make my way back to my home, I cannot stop thinking of her. I turn my open palm up, studying it a moment and remembering the feel of her skin against mine.

If I were human, I would court her according to the ways of her people. I would kiss her and ask her to be mine. I would bind myself to her: body, mind, heart, and soul.

Something inside me is pulled to her, and I feel as if she is meant to be mine.

But how could this be? It would be impossible. We are too

different. I can never give her the life that a human male could. I cannot give her a home, family, children…

I'm so lost in my thoughts that I don't notice my father is nearby until his voice booms in my head. *"Where were you?"*

"Hunting," I reply quickly. The only excuse I could come up with on short notice.

"Then, where is your catch for the day?"

"I was unsuccessful," I tell him.

"Princess Luriel is coming soon to see you," he says. *"Do not forget."*

Reluctantly, I nod. *"I won't, Father."*

"Good." He claps a hand on my shoulder. *"Now come join me and your brother for dinner. We waited for you."*

When I follow him into the dining hall, I take a seat next to Toren. We listen as father tells us about his day.

After we're done, Toren follows me to my room. He crosses his arms over his chest. *"Where were you really?"*

I could lie, but I won't. Not to Toren. *"With Halla."*

His eyes widen. *"Are you mad?"*

"What's wrong with spending time with her?"

"It's dangerous," he counters.

"Halla isn't dangerous, Toren."

"Not her," he agrees. *"Others of her kind. Many of them are afraid of us. And fear can easily lead to hate."*

I sigh. *"You have nothing to worry about. I'm careful when I'm on the surface."*

He claps a hand on my shoulder. *"I just worry for you. Besides, if Father finds out you've been spending time with a human, he'll be furious."*

I shrug. *"Then… I will just have to make sure he does not find out."*

Toren sighs. *"I do not think it will be that easy to hide it from him."* He turns to go to his own room, pausing at my door a moment. *"If you're going to lie to him, at least think of a better excuse beside 'hunting.'"*

He's right. If I'm going to continue spending time with Halla, I'll need to think of a better excuse for why I'm gone most of the day. The last thing I need is Father getting suspicious and investigating where I am.

CHAPTER 10

HALLA

It's been almost a month since I started swimming every day with Errik. A light knock at my door announces my brother, Gerold. He greets me with a smile, but I read the sadness in his eyes and the stress in his posture. The city is still in ruins after the dragon's fire, but the people are doing their best to pick up the pieces and move on.

"How are things in the rest of the kingdom?"

Gerold slips one arm behind my back and another under my knees to carry me down to the dining hall for the first meal. "They are as well as expected."

His tone makes me worry. "What's wrong, Gerold? You can tell me."

He sighs as we make our way down the stairs. "I have good news and bad news." I tense. "Which do you want first?"

"The bad," I immediately answer. I've always been one to face the grim truth head-on. "Then, the good."

He sets me down at the table and pushes in my chair

before he takes the seat across from me. He must have terrible news because I notice that he stalls for time by offering me the toast and butter before answering.

I push the food away and narrow my eyes. "You're stalling, Gerold. Tell me."

"The kingdom's coffers are nearly empty."

I blink at him, stunned. "But I thought—"

"The damage done by the dragon wrecked us, Halla. We've used much of what we had in reserve to begin rebuilding. Because so many were affected, I cannot raise taxes on those who have already lost so much."

He's right. "What are we going to do?"

He clenches his jaw and sits back in his chair. "I've received an offer."

His tone makes me pause. I bring my tea to my lips and take a sip. "What kind of offer?"

"For your hand."

Bewildered, I set down the cup, which clatters against the saucer. "Who? Do they—do they know about my... condition?"

He nods. "It's King Henrick of Arnafell. Their kingdom is wealthy. Marriage with him would—"

"Arnafell?" I straighten. "You cannot be serious, Gerold. I'll freeze to death up there. I cannot live in such a miserable place. Please tell me that is *not* the good news."

He shakes his head. "It's not."

I collapse back in my chair. "Well, thank goodness for that. What is the good news, then?"

"I've heard word from the Fae. They have agreed to send a Healer."

"They have?" I try but fail to temper the hope in my question.

"Yes," Gerold replies. "This is a very big change from their usual stance toward humans. They wanted nothing to do with us at all until recently."

"I remember."

His expression sobers. "About King Henrick... you do not have to accept him. I've heard he is a sound leader and skilled in battle, but I've heard little else about him since he ascended to the throne after his father's death. We can always appeal to one of our allies to ask for a loan to rebuild if you refuse Henrick's offer."

Gerold's words are meant to be reassuring, but I hear what he does not say. *What if our allies refuse to help us?*

I sit back, considering. I have always wanted only to serve our people and our kingdom. If marriage to Henrick would help to rebuild, I do not know that I can refuse King Henrick simply because I dislike the idea of living in the frozen north.

"What are your plans for the day?" Gerold asks, ripping me from my thoughts. "Swimming again?"

I nod, then look down at my legs. Focusing all my efforts, I lift my left foot slightly, then my right. Gerold gasps. "When did you discover you could do that?"

"A few days ago. I was able to kick a bit more in the water yesterday as well."

He grins. "Althea was right. The water is doing you some good."

My expression falls. "I just hope the Fae Healer can help with the rest."

He takes my hand, squeezing it gently. "Me too."

I open my mouth to tell him about Errik but stop. I'm not sure how my brother would feel about me spending time with a Merman. I do not think Gerold would disapprove, but I'm not sure, and I don't want him to demand I stop spending time with Errik. I enjoy his company. This past month I've spent with him has been one of the happiest in my life, even despite my injury.

It's more than that, however. I look forward to seeing him every day.

As I make my way down to the shore, I'm anxious to see him. I scan the water, searching for any sign that he's nearby. When I notice his glowing blue eyes in the distance, I smile and wave.

He waves back and swims toward me.

"You're late," he teases.

My heart flutters as his gaze holds mine and a devastatingly handsome smile curves his lips.

I lift my eyes to the sun. "No, I'm not. I'm early."

We've been meeting daily for almost a month. We swim for several hours every day as I strengthen my upper body and do my best to move my legs to regain more function.

I remove my shirt and pants, leaving me in only my undergarments. No one ever swims along this part of the shoreline, so I've never had to worry about discovery when I swim like this. Errik and I are always the only ones out here.

He told me once that his people think nothing of nudity. That the Mer women only cover their breasts because they hate the way land dwellers stare at them. However, I cannot help but notice Errik's eyes tracing my form now and then when he thinks I am not looking.

I'd like to think that he finds me attractive, but it's more likely that he finds me strange. He has commented many times on the differences between me and a Mer.

I push off from my chair, and his strong arms catch me before I hit the rocky shore. His skin is warm against mine, and my heart hammers as his mouth curves into a handsome smile.

"Careful," he gently chastises. "We talked about this. It is not good for you to simply throw yourself onto the ground."

"I didn't," I reply with a grin. "I knew you would catch me."

He laughs as he carries me into the water, cradling me to his chest with one arm while he uses the other to push himself along the sand. I've heard that Mer are much stronger than humans, I believe it now. He has superhuman strength, and holds me as if I weigh nothing.

Once we enter the water, he releases his hold on me, and I already miss his arms around my form.

I arch a teasing brow. "I'm going to beat you today."

He chuckles. "Is that so?"

"Yes."

I glance over my shoulder at the rock island we usually swim to. We now call it *our* rock. Without warning, I start toward it, making long strokes with my arms and trying my best to kick my feet behind me in the process.

He swims beside me, his expression serious.

I try but fail to suppress a grin. I know very well that he can swim much faster than me, but he lets me think I am making him work to beat me at this game we play every day. He's thoughtful, so I do not call him on his ruse. Besides, I love swimming with him. This is the best part of my day—the time that we spend together.

A ship catches my eye in the distance. The large white sail a stark contrast to the blue of the ocean. My mouth drifts open when I notice the golden banner with a falcon crest waving in the breeze. It's a Skallog ship.

Errik swims up beside me, following my line of sight. "Word has spread among the Mer to avoid that ship," he says. "The males have been threatening to kill any of my people if we get too near."

"Why?"

"They say Prince Edwyrd's new bride is afraid we will try to drown them."

I still. "Prince Edwyrd?" Although I did not love him, his rejection of our betrothal after my injury still hurt.

Errik's hand cups my cheek, drawing my attention to him. "What's wrong, Halla?" His glowing blue eyes search mine in concern. "Why are you upset?"

"Prince Edwyrd was my betrothed," I explain. "He's the one who rejected me."

Errik wraps his arms around me, pulling me close to his chest as we float in the water. "Oh, Halla, I'm so sorry. He did not deserve your love. He—"

"I did not love him," I answer quickly. "But his rejection made me feel..."

"Feel what?" Errik asks.

I lift my gaze to his. "I'd rather not talk about it. All right?"

Reluctantly, he nods.

CHAPTER 11

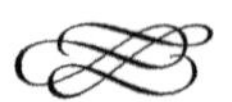

ERRIK

As I watch Prince Edwyrd's ship sail away in the distance, anger roils deep inside me. He was a fool to break off his betrothal to Halla. That he could so easily do this simply because of her injury tells me that he would never have been worthy of her. If she were mine, I would never let her go.

Ever since she saw his ship, she's been pushing herself harder than I've ever seen her do before. She has swum several laps back and forth between the rocks and the shoreline, bringing her to the point of exhaustion.

I watch her float on her back, staring up at the sky. Her chest rises and falls as she struggles to catch her breath.

"Shall we go back?" I ask, concerned.

"Not yet. I want to do another lap."

I frown. "You push yourself too hard, Halla. You should rest."

Her blue eyes narrow. "You're just worried I'll beat you, aren't you?"

I laugh. "You've discovered the truth."

A wide smile splits her face. "I'm going to swim to that far rock formation, Errik. I think I can make it."

My expression sobers. I know which one she is talking about; this rock lies very far out to sea. The waves are much stronger there, and I worry she could be hurt.

"I do not think that would be wise."

"Why not?"

"We've been swimming for hours. You're exhausted. Your arms were already shaking when we swam the last lap, and your legs—" I stop short. She hates when I mention her disability, but I know that I must. "I do not think you will make it."

She narrows her eyes. "The first thing you should learn about me, Errik, is that I never back down from a challenge."

I have obviously offended her, and I open my mouth to assuage her, but she turns and starts for the rocks. I'm surprised by how quickly she can swim without the use of her legs. I doubt I'd be as fast if I were unable to use my tail.

I join her, keeping pace. She grins at me as she slices her hands through the water in that strange way humans help propel themselves forward while swimming. "Having a hard time keeping up?"

I arch a brow. "I am Mer. My body was made to move through the water. You'll have to do better than that if you plan to beat me to the rocks."

To my complete and utter surprise, she accelerates. She still isn't swimming faster than me, but her pace is impressive, nonetheless.

A giant wave rushes toward us, and she takes a deep breath and dives beneath the surface. When she comes up on the other side, she draws in great gulping breaths of air.

I gaze at her in concern. "We should turn back, Halla."

"No," she snaps before diving beneath another wave.

I clench my jaw at her stubbornness. It's going to get her killed someday.

I slip beneath the wave, watching her struggle to swim. Without the full use of her legs, her arms must work harder to compensate, and it is easy to see that she is already tiring when we're not even halfway there.

When we surface, I request again, "We should go back."

"No, I can make it, Errik. I know I can."

Her face is set in a mask of determination as she presses on.

Another wave approaches quickly, and she dives, but not soon enough. The swell catches her, and I watch in horror as she goes tumbling underwater.

She cries out, and a stream of bubbles escapes her mouth along with all of her air.

I pull her into my arms and seal my mouth over hers, breathing air into her lungs.

When I pull back, she studies me. Her scarlet hair rises around her head, swaying with the tide. I gather her in my arms and swim to the surface. Her arms tremble with exhaustion as her hold weakens.

I lean down and whisper in her ear, "It's all right, Halla. You can relax. I've got you."

She sags against me as I swim us back to our rock island near the castle.

Carefully, I carry her onto the shore. I prop us both against a rock to sit up. She is quiet, her gaze fixed on the horizon across the sea. A tear slips down her cheek, but she quickly brushes it away.

I take her hand. "What is wrong?"

"Nothing," she denies.

"Halla. Whatever it is, you can tell me. Is it Edwyrd? Is it because you saw his ship?"

She turns away, but even from this angle, I can see

another tear roll down her cheek. "He rejected me because of my condition, Errik." Her voice quavers. "I thought I was getting stronger."

I squeeze her hand. "You *are* getting stronger. Every day. I can see it."

"Every day I keep hoping… praying that I'll somehow be able to walk again, but I still cannot, Errik. Prince Edwyrd didn't want me because he thinks I'm broken… and I'm starting to believe that he's right."

I gather her to my chest, holding her close as I run my fingers through the long scarlet strands of her hair. I whisper in her ear. "You are not broken, Halla." I pull back just enough to drop my forehead gently to hers. "Edwyrd was a fool to reject you. You are the strongest, bravest, and most beautiful female I have ever known. Any male who cannot see this, does not deserve you."

I'm completely mesmerized as her blue eyes search mine. Her gaze drops to my mouth and my heart hammers as she leans in. The warmth of her breath fans across my skin and I go still.

Gently, her lips brush against mine in a featherlight touch.

"Halla!" her brother calls out, startling us both.

She pulls back, her eyes wide. "I'm sorry, Errik. I shouldn't have done that."

"Halla, I—"

"I have to go." She starts to swim toward the shore, but stops and looks over her shoulder. "I'll see you tomorrow?"

There is nothing I'd rather do more than see her again. Tomorrow, the day after… and every day for the rest of my life. "Yes."

CHAPTER 12

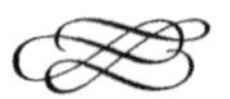

HALLA

As I make my way back to the shore, I find Gerold waiting for me beside my chair. I smile to myself when I feel the barest hint of Errik's fin brush against my arm. He thinks I don't know that he always escorts me back to the shore.

I sigh in frustration. I cannot believe I almost kissed him. I have to protect my heart. Errik and I cannot be together. It would never work.

And yet… I cannot stay away from him, and I certainly can't stop thinking of him.

A small splash draws my attention and I see his tail emerge from the water and then disappear as he dives back beneath the surface.

Gerold must notice it too because when he helps me into my chair, he arches a brow. "Was that a Mer tail I saw just now?"

"Yes. His name is Errik. He's been swimming with me."

"Errik," he repeats the name to himself as if committing it

to memory. "Is this your mysterious Merman that rescued you?" he asks teasingly.

I laugh. "Actually, he is."

Gerold's expression falls. "Well, why have I not met him yet? I would like to thank him for saving my dear sister."

"His people know that many of ours are afraid of them. So, they try to avoid us… for the most part."

"Understandable," he murmurs. His gaze slides to mine. "I have news to share with you."

"What is it?"

"King Henrick will be arriving soon. He is coming to meet with you. To see if you might be agreeable to marrying him."

I turn to my brother. "Does he know I'm still unable to walk?"

Gerold nods.

"And… he still wants to marry me?"

"Yes."

I blink at Gerold, stunned.

He takes my hand. "Not everyone is shallow like Prince Edwyrd."

I give him a faint smile.

He continues. "Remember: you do not have to marry King Henrick if you do not wish. But… it would not hurt to meet with him. If nothing else, perhaps he could become an ally. Besides being known for how cold it is there, his kingdom is also known for its wealth."

I swallow thickly and allow my gaze to sweep over our city as Gerold pushes my chair up the path back to the castle. Everywhere there is still evidence of the damage wrought by the dragon. Our people work tirelessly to rebuild, but our coffers are low. A marriage to Henrick would be a boon to our kingdom.

It would also help us to fortify our defenses. It is known

far and wide that our city has suffered greatly. Gerold is constantly worried about the threat of pirates.

When I reach my room, I wheel myself out to the balcony overlooking the sea. I cast my gaze out to the water. Silver moonlight shines down upon the waves, casting shimmering reflections across the surface. The crisp saline breeze blows gently through my hair, and I sigh heavily as my thoughts turn to Errik.

I wish I were Mer or that he was human. I almost kissed him today. I certainly wanted to. But we're too different, he and I. A Mer and a human cannot be together. Not like that anyway. Besides… why would he want me? Errik is the most handsome man I've ever seen; I'm sure he could have his pick of beautiful mermaids.

I know it would be impossible between us, but I cannot help but dream.

CHAPTER 13

ERRIK

When I reach the palace, I find Father and Toren waiting for me. Toren's eyes flash with warning as I swim up to them.

Father narrows his eyes. *"Where have you been?"*

I could try to convince him I was hunting again, but it's an excuse I've already used too many times. Sighing heavily, I offer him a half-truth instead. *"I was meeting with someone."*

He blinks several times, obviously stunned by my answer. *"Who?"*

Toren's eyes go wide and he shakes his head softly behind Father, trying to warn me against telling him.

"A female," I reply, intentionally vague.

Father's brow furrows deeply. *"Who?"*

I shrug. *"She is not from here. Her people live along the coast."* It's not a complete lie. Halla *does* live on the coastline.

Father studies me a moment, considering. *"You are a prince, Errik. The heir to our kingdom."* He places a hand on my shoulder. *"If this were not so, I would not care who you choose to bond with. But as the future leader of our people, you have... other things to consider."*

"Father, I—"

He raises his hands in a bid to allow him to continue. *"An alliance with the kingdom of Itlana would help ensure peace among our people for generations to come."*

"We already have peace with them, Father. We have a treaty."

"Yes, but not one tied by blood. Their kingdom is strong, like ours. An alliance strengthened through a bonding would ensure our kingdom is protected against any enemies." He pauses. *"Princess Luriel will be here soon to meet with you."*

His gaze drops to my tail. *"If you are blessed, perhaps your fate markings will begin to glow the moment you meet her. That is what happened shortly after I met your mother. My tail did not glow right away, mind you. But before it did, I knew, Errik. I knew your mother was my fated one."*

He claps one hand on my shoulder and another on Toren's. *"I pray that it will be so with you and your brother as well."* His gaze slides to mine. *"Princess Luriel is intelligent, beautiful, and beloved by her people. Even without the fate markings, I believe she would make an excellent match for you."*

My thoughts turn to Halla. I wish desperately that she could be mine. But she is human. It would never work between us. Even so, I cannot stop the longing in my heart as I think of her.

When morning comes, I make my way back to the surface. I cannot stop thinking of my father's words. I will have to meet with Princess Luriel soon. The thought fills me with dread.

I want Halla as my mate. No one else. I glance at my tail,

praying it will light with the fate markings when I see Halla. But it's impossible.

As soon as I reach the shoreline, I notice her empty chair already on the beach. Panic stills my heart as my gaze scans the water and I do not see her.

"Halla!" I call out.

"Over here," she replies, and I realize her voice is coming from the small island rock formation we often sunbathe on.

I immediately swim toward it, surprised when I find her sitting up on the beach, her gaze fixed on the water with a faraway look. "Halla?"

Her eyes meet mine, full of tears.

I drag myself up onto the sand, and move to her side. I take her hand in my own. "What's wrong?"

"King Henrick of Arnafell has asked for my hand."

My heart stutters and stops in my chest.

"He's on his way here even now to propose."

"Do you want to bond with him?" I ask, both anxious and fearful of her answer.

She shrugs. "I… do not know."

I search her eyes. "What do you mean?"

"Our kingdom has run out of money. The rebuilding has nearly emptied our treasury. Arnafell is a wealthy kingdom, and King Henrick has offered to help us in exchange for my hand." She looks down at her legs. "He knows about my injury and he does not care. More than that though… he might be my only chance at having children—a family."

A deep ache settles in my chest. I cannot bear to think of her with another male. "Have you ever even met him?"

"No. But I've heard that he is brave and very handsome."

With great difficulty, I manage to suppress the snarl rumbling my chest.

She turns to me, her blue eyes searching mine. "What do you think I should do?"

I don't want her to bond with King Henrick. I want her to be mine. However, I cannot tell her this. She is human and I am… not. It would never work. So, instead, I force a platitude past my lips. "You should do whatever you believe will make you happy."

She lowers her gaze, and her expression is one I recognize as disappointment, but I do not understand why.

"Errik, I—"

"Errik!" Toren calls out, startling us both.

I whip my head toward my brother, and so does Halla. He swims closer, and I notice she moves behind me, her hands on my shoulders.

I glance back at her. "It is only my brother, Toren."

Her cheeks flush deep red. "But I'm half-naked, Errik."

Her words make me wonder. She's never had a problem undressing in front of me. Why now my brother? "Nudity is not—"

"Frowned upon among your people. I know. But it is for mine."

My heart stutters and stops. She is reacting this way because she trusts me and only me to see her partially clothed. My chest swells with pride at the thought. I tip my chin up high as my brother approaches.

His eyes widen when he notices her behind me.

"Toren," I begin. "This is Halla. Halla, this is my younger brother, Toren."

"It is nice to meet you." He dips his chin in greeting.

"You too," she replies.

He shifts his gaze to me pointedly. "Father is looking for you."

"I will be there shortly. First, I must escort Halla back to shore."

He purses his lips. "Do not take long. If he discovers you here, he'll be angry."

I nod, and Toren swims away.

Halla places a hand on my forearm, drawing my attention to her. "I'll be fine, Errik. You should go before you get in trouble."

I don't want to leave her, but I also know I must speak with Father. If I do not go to him now, he might find me here. He'll be furious if he does.

Hearing Halla speak of King Henrick made me realize something. I cannot bond with Princess Luriel. I cannot offer myself to her when my heart already belongs to Halla. I love Halla. Even if she can never be mine, I cannot bind myself to another.

"Will I see you tomorrow?" she asks.

"Yes." I take both her hands in mine as I stare deep into her lovely blue eyes. "I will be here."

She nods, and I watch her return to shore. I curl my hands into fists at my side as devastation and jealousy war within me. She should be mine, not King Henrick's. Why was I cursed to be Mer? Why could I not have been human like her? I could have asked her to bond with me then. To be my mate and remain by her side forever.

Arnafell lies across the sea. Thick islands of floating ice surround the kingdom most of the year, making travel and even swimming treacherous. If she marries King Henrick, I'll never see her again.

As I make my way home, I cannot stop thinking of her words. She wants a family—children. Even if she somehow wished to be with me, I do not think I could give her this. We are two different species. I've never heard of a Mer having a child with a human. Yes, there are rumors and myths, but that is all they are. I doubt such a pairing is even possible. If it were, could it result in healthy children?

I look down at my mating pouch. I've seen enough human men to know our male anatomy is similar. Theirs is always protruding however, whereas ours only protrudes from our body when we are ready to mate. My *stav* is a bit larger and thicker than a human's, but that does not mean—

"Errik," a familiar voice calls, startling me.

I turn to find Dorin—father's advisor—swimming toward me. He places a hand on my arm, the corners of his eyes crinkling as he smiles at me. *"Princess Luriel is here. She is anxious to meet you."*

I lower my gaze. *"I have decided that I cannot—"*

He raises his hands in a placating gesture. *"Before you do anything rash, Errik... This is merely a meeting. I'm sure she's curious to know if you may be a fated match. That is all."*

I sigh heavily. I want Halla and no other. But I do not know how it could possibly work between us. Deep down, part of me hopes that Luriel and I are fated. Then I would know for certain that Halla is not meant to be mine, even though every instinct insists otherwise. My stubborn heart refuses to give up despite that we are different species.

"All right. Take me to her."

Besides, my fate marks have not glowed since I've met Halla.

I turn to Dorin. *"The fate marks... Father said his did not appear for my mother right away. Is it common for there to be a delay?"*

He nods. *"Most often, the bond starts with a knowing deep within. Your soul recognizes its other half before the fate marks appear."*

Hope fills me. *"Has this ever happened with someone... outside of our species?"*

He stops and turns to me with a wary expression. *"Why do you ask this?"*

I'm not ready to tell him the truth just yet. *"I'm simply curious. I've heard rumors all my life and wondered."*

He clenches his jaw. *"The last pairing I heard of happened many years ago. It was... terrible. The man killed himself not long after the child was born."*

Last pairing? Child? My heart stutters. *"Tell me what happened."*

"You must tell no one." He narrows his eyes. *"I'm not entirely sure how you even heard rumors, but you must not repeat them. We hide such stories to discourage others from following this path. Do you understand?"*

Numbly, I nod.

"Many years ago, a Merman fell in love with a human woman. He claimed that they were fated. They had a child born with human legs."

"And the child was healthy?" I demand anxiously.

He nods. *"However, neither the child nor the mother could be with the Merman. After a time, they grew apart, and... the woman moved on, taking the child with her. The man killed himself not long after. He could not bear being parted from his mate and his daughter."*

"What happened to the child?"

"We do not know. She may not even know what she is," he explains. *"That is why we do not speak of this, Errik. Humans are not like us. They do not mate for life. We do not want to encourage any Mer to follow this example."*

I understand why he and my father have kept this secret. However, instead of discouraging me, the story has had the opposite effect. It has given me hope where I had none before.

Now, I no longer dread my meeting with Luriel, for I already know in my heart that she is *not* my fated one. Halla is.

When I swim into the throne room, I find her floating before my father. She turns to me with a charming smile. Her golden hair fans around her head like a glowing halo and her lavender eyes appraise me. I greet her warmly but feel nothing. No attraction, nor pull of my soul to hers in any way.

Our meeting has only deepened my conviction. Halla is meant to be mine. I am certain of it. Now, I just need to find out if she feels the same way.

CHAPTER 14

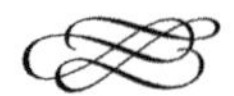

HALLA

All night, I dreamed of Errik. I cannot stop thinking about him and our conversation yesterday. When I asked him what I should do about King Henrick, he merely advised me to do what makes me happy.

Sadness settles in my chest. Errik must not have feelings for me like I thought he might. If he did, surely he would have said something. If our situations were reversed, I believe I would have, at least.

Then again, maybe not. We spend time together every day, but I've never told him how I feel. Deep down, I fear he would only reject me. I am human, not Mer. And, why would he want me when I am broken?

King Henrick, however, does not seem deterred by my condition.

The first of the sun's rays filter in from the balcony as Gerold walks into my room. He greets me warmly. "King Henrick has just arrived. His ships were seen down at the docks. You should dress quickly; I will send for you once he is here."

I'm so nervous, I can hardly think. The man who may be my future husband is here. Compulsively, my thoughts return to Errik. I wish that I were Mer, or that he were human. I love him, but our love cannot be. Besides, I doubt he would ever return my affections. And if I truly care about my people and our kingdom, I will push aside my selfish desires for a man I could never possibly have, and do what is best for them.

I bathe and then dress. Althea comes in to check on me as she does every morning and night.

She takes hold of the sole of my left foot. "Push as hard as you can against me, Halla."

I grit my teeth and concentrate all my energy and effort on my task. My body is slow to respond but eventually obeys. After I exercise the other foot, her lips quirk up in a faint smile. "There is some improvement."

"But not much." I voice the words she does not.

She nods, taking my hand and squeezing gently. "The Fae have many methods of healing. Once they send their Healer, I have great hope that they will be able to help you, Halla."

"At least King Henrick does not seem to care if I am whole or not," I say, trying to find the bright spot in all of this suffering. "That bodes well, does it not?"

She smiles. "Yes, it certainly does."

"Althea, you have traveled far and wide, have you not?"

She nods.

"Have you ever—" I stop short, uncertain how to ask what I want. Drawing in a deep breath, I force the words past my lips. "Have you ever heard of a human bonding to a Mer?"

Her eyes snap up to mine and her expression falters. "Why do you ask this?"

"I... was simply curious," I lie. "That's all."

She sits on the edge of the bed, clasping her hands tightly together in her lap as she straightens. Her gaze meets mine evenly. "I have heard of this. But, as far as I know, such pairings do not end well."

"What do you mean?"

"One trapped by the sea and the other forced to live on land." Something akin to sadness flashes briefly behind her eyes. "How could such a bonding ever withstand that kind of permanent separation? It would be doomed to fail from the start, Halla." Her gaze holds mine. "Do you understand?"

I swallow against the lump in my throat. "Yes."

"Come now." She forces a cheery smile to her face. "Let us go meet this King Henrick. I have heard he is a good man."

I'm anxious, and I don't like the idea of waiting in my room. So, instead of waiting for Gerold to come back and help me, I wheel myself to the door and push down my pride as I ask one of the guards to carry me down the stairs to the throne room, where I know Gerold will be receiving King Henrick.

As soon as the guard carries me through the doorway, Gerold's lips tip up in a smirk. "I knew you'd be down here as soon as you were dressed."

The guard gently helps me into my chair, and I wheel myself to Gerold's side. I'm too nervous to conjure a witty reply or joke. I push my hands into my lap, wringing the fabric of my dress as I try but fail to calm my nerves.

"Is this what you do all day? Sit here and do nothing?" I cannot help but tease him.

"What are you talking about?" He laughs. "I'm rarely in this room. I'm only here now to wait for your suitor's arrival. For *you*, I might add."

"For us," I remind him.

He frowns, the mood between us somber now. "You know you need not do anything you do not wish. Please tell me that you understand that, my dear sister."

"I do," I reply, thankful that I have a brother who loves me more than he loves wealth. "Even if I refuse his hand, we can still ask him for help."

Gerold nods, but it is easy to read the fatigue in his expression. The weight of the entire kingdom rests on his shoulders. I cannot imagine how terrible a burden it must be. "I know we should, but I do not know how," he admits. "I am dreading it, to be honest. I feel like I've failed our people, Halla."

It is rare that my brother is not in a teasing or joking mood. He must be deeply worried that he is not a good king if he is admitting his fears aloud.

He continues. "The dragon's attack has left us vulnerable. Whatever cannons were not destroyed, their munitions have almost all been spent."

"Can we still defend the city against pirates?"

"No," he replies soberly. "That is what keeps me awake at night. We never needed to worry about an attack before, but now that we are weak, I fear it is only a matter of time before they come to prey on us."

I cannot deny that this news unnerves me. No wonder my brother appears so worn of late.

I take his hand, drawing his attention back to me. "You are a wise, fit ruler, Gerold. I know that you work every day to help with the cleanup and oversee the reconstruction of this city. It is not your fault that the dragon came, but you are doing everything you can to restore Solwyck to the best of your abilities. Anyone with honor will recognize this. If they are truly our friends and allies, they will understand that you are asking not because you failed as a king, but because you are humble enough to seek aid for your people."

A ghost of a smile curls his lips. “Did I ever tell you that you give wise council, my dear sister?”

“Never.” I grin. “But you may start now.”

CHAPTER 15

HALLA

One of the guards enters, interrupting our conversation. He bows low. "Forgive me, Your Highnesses, but King Henrick has arrived."

My heart slams in my throat. I push my hands into my lap to still their shaking as I tip my chin up to receive our most welcome guest.

"Show him in," Gerold orders.

The doors open, and my mouth drifts open as King Henrick appears. He is indeed as handsome as they say. He has a proud, square jaw that could cut glass, and blond hair—the color so light it appears almost white—piercing blue eyes, and a tall, broad-shouldered physique. His body is heavily muscled.

Despite his attractiveness, he cannot rival Errik. Helplessly, I wish he were somehow here.

My brother stands to greet him. "Welcome, King Henrick. I am King Gerold, and this is my sister, Princess Halla. We are glad you have arrived safely."

"Thank you. I am happy to be here." King Henrick dips his chin in a subdued bow. His eyes snap to me, and I still as he pins me with an intense gaze. He walks toward me and drops to one knee. "Forgive my directness, Your Highness, but you are more beautiful than I was told."

I smile, pleasantly surprised by his words. "Thank you."

His gaze drops to my legs. "All have heard of your bravery. It is a shame you are now broken."

My head jerks back at his blunt words. "I..." I trail off, unsure of how to respond.

He continues. "Perhaps my Healers can examine whether anything can be done."

"I... would appreciate that, my Lord," I reply, trying to be polite.

We go to the dining hall, offering him and his men refreshments after a long journey. Henrick sits across from me. I'm surprised when the food arrives and he rests his arms on either side of his plate, along with the rest of his men.

Instead of using the cutlery provided, they all use their hands, tearing into their food and eating loudly. Gerold's eyes dart to mine.

Henrick lifts his gaze to me and smiles before shoving another oversized mouthful of bread in his mouth. Using his other hand, he rips off a piece of steak with his teeth, that appear strangely sharp—almost like fangs.

I glance down at my fork and knife and begin politely cutting into my food. I do not want to be rude, so I pretend that his way of eating is not strange to me. Gerold does the same.

Henrick's eyes dart to me then my brother. "I like what I

see. My offer still stands. I will give you the wealth to rebuild Solwyck in exchange for your sister's hand."

Gerold faces me. "The decision is not mine, Your Highness. It belongs to Halla."

Henrick's brow furrows deeply. "Fine. Let us spend time together this evening after dinner." His blue eyes study me. "You may ask me whatever you wish, Princess. I am an open book."

"Thank you." I smile politely. "You may do the same."

Once dinner is over, I wheel into the garden while Henrick follows beside me. The gardens overlook the ocean. They are lovely, dotted with flowering bushes carrying vibrant red-and-blue flowers. I love the long, trailing green vines with tiny purple glowing blossoms most. They drape over the garden walls, swaying in the breeze like living curtains. They were planted by my mother, and I am once again glad that these gardens were spared from the dragon's fire.

Henrick walks beside me, studying the many wide, flat stones Gerold has had placed along the path for my chair to maneuver easily.

"I can have the castle fitted with whatever you need to move with your chair," he says. "I will do all that I can to make your life easier."

Surprised by his thoughtful words, I thank him.

He nods. "It is the least I can do."

I stop and turn to face him. "You are so certain you want me, Your Highness?"

His gaze rakes over my form, and he nods firmly. "I need a future queen and someone to carry my heirs. You are lovely. Despite your broken body, I assume you may still be bred."

My eyes widen, and my breath hitches in my throat.

"Your... Highness?" I hedge, wondering if I've heard him wrong. "Did you ask if... I can be *bred?*"

"Yes," he replies.

"Like a horse?" I ask, agitation seeping into my tone.

He clasps his hands behind his back and cocks his head to the side. "Forgive me. You find my manner of speaking blunt, I assume."

"Yes."

"It is my way—the way of the north. Life is hard in the ice and snow, and we do not have time for flowery words or flattery." He pauses. "Will this be a problem for you?"

"I—" I stop short, uncertain of how to reply. "What about love?" I finally ask. "Is there any place for such emotion in the northern lands?"

His gaze holds mine for a moment before he responds, "I will be completely honest with you, Princess. Will that be acceptable to you?"

"Of course. Please, continue."

He takes a seat on a bench beside me, studying me for a moment. "You are known for your intelligence, Princess Halla. A quality very valuable to have in one's mate. And you are even more beautiful than the rumors I have heard. I have lands, ships, a castle, wealth, but I lack a wife. I cannot give you love, but I vow that I will never lie to you.

"I understand that many princes and kings have affairs, but that is not my way. I promise I will provide you with a good home and whatever you desire. I ask only in return that you rule by my side, give me at least two heirs, and never deny me your bed. Is this acceptable to you?"

He must recognize the hesitation in my eyes because he adds, "I know your kingdom's coffers are nearly empty. I would give your brother whatever he needs and more to rebuild Solwyck, but only in exchange for what I ask—your hand."

He pauses to let his words sink in. "I doubt you will receive a better offer considering your situation, Princess. You are beautiful, but your body is not whole. I understand politics, and I know that if not for the dragon fire and your accident, you would never even consider me. Yet I promise you that our kingdom will be ruled wisely. I do not allow feelings to get in the way of logic; that is what makes me a good ruler." He stands. "Think about what I have said."

He starts to turn away but stills as if thinking better of it. He takes my hand, and I'm in too much shock at his words to pull away. He brings my hand to his mouth and presses a chaste kiss on the back.

His blue eyes search mine. "I suspect you appreciate affectionate gestures. I will try to remember this in the future if you wish." He dips his chin. "We will speak again in the morning."

As he walks away, I'm left gaping. I've never been spoken to so bluntly. While I appreciate honesty, I've never realized how important the simple niceties between people are until now. When you strip away the little things, you are left with only the hollow darkness of… nothing but stark and hard truth.

That is what I sense in his eyes. No cruelty, no malice, no kindness or gentleness there. Simply truth. No emotion.

Can I really spend the rest of my life with a husband who speaks without passion and wants me only for the heirs I can bear? A man who thinks nothing of telling me that I am broken?

My thoughts turn to Errik. I wish he were here. I miss his shining eyes, his bright smile when he sees me, his kind words, and the way he touches me so carefully and so tenderly when he helps me to and from my chair.

Tears sting my eyes and blur my vision. I'm too upset to

call for one of the guards to carry me up the stairs to my room. I don't want anyone to see me like this.

It's not as if King Henrick is cruel; he is simply blunt and honest. So why am I crying? Why am I so devastated? Though Gerold assured me I do not have to marry him, King Henrick was right. What other offers will I have?

None.

If I want to do what's best for the people of Solwyck, I will marry him, and he will give Gerold whatever he needs to rebuild our kingdom. The people will have food and all that they desire. Solwyck can become a bright and shining city once again.

I make my way toward the sea. Stripping off my dress, I push out of the chair and drag my body into the water. It is dark, and the moon is only half full, but it casts enough light to guide my swim to the rocky island—mine and Errik's. I drag myself onto the hard stone and sand, and curl up on my side.

Errik's image resurfaces in my mind, and I cannot stop crying because I know he can never be mine. A broken sob escapes me, the sound swallowed by the wind, as I cry my anguish to the stars.

CHAPTER 16

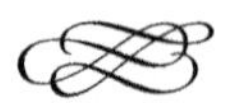

ERRIK

All night, my thoughts kept returning to Halla. I cannot stop thinking about her proposal from King Henrick. I can hardly stand the mere thought of another man touching her.

I want her to be mine. I do not care if she is human; I love her, and I am desperate to tell her.

It is difficult to remain here when I want to leave and find Halla as soon as possible. But, I understand that relations between our kingdom and Luriel's are important. I cannot risk offending them by leaving before we have breakfast. I'm already risking offense by planning to refuse Luriel's hand.

As soon as I'm able to leave, I head for Solwyck. When I break through the surface by the shore, I catch a faint hint of Halla's scent on the breeze.

Flaring my nostrils, I follow the trail to our rock where we swim every day. A broken sob is quickly swallowed by the wind. It stills my heart, for I know it is Halla.

I rush toward her, swimming as fast as I can. When I

reach the rock, my heart slams against my ribs. She is curled up on the surface, crying.

I pull myself toward her and gather her into my arms. "Halla? What is wrong?"

Her blue eyes turn to me, brimming with despairing tears.

I brush the hair back from her face and cup her chin. "Are you hurt?" I ask, panicked when she does not answer right away.

"No." Her voice quavers. "I am broken."

"What are you talking about?"

"That's what *he* said."

"Who?"

"King Henrick," she murmurs. "He said I was broken, and that no one will want me but him. He will give Gerold whatever he needs to rebuild Solwyck, but only if I marry him." She draws in a deep breath. "How can I refuse him when he will help our people?"

Anger heats my core. She is as selfless as she is brave to even consider bonding to a man who would speak so cruelly to her just for the sake of her people.

"How can I be selfish and say no if—"

"Don't marry him, Halla. If you need wealth, I will find it for you."

She blinks up at me.

"Do you know how much treasure lies at the bottom of the sea? My people have no use for it. We do not trade in coins or fine jewels. My brother and I will bring all you need and more." I comb my hand through her hair and press a tender kiss to her forehead. I will risk my father's wrath by doing this, rather than watch her marry a man she does not want because her kingdom needs money. "Do not marry a man who would speak to you this way. He does not see you for what you are."

She studies me. "What am I?"

"You are intelligent, brave, beautiful, and strong. Where others would have given up, you persevere, fighting to regain what you have lost. In doing so, you have become so much stronger, Halla. You are the fiercest person I know." I touch her cheek. "Any man who cannot see this does not deserve your hand."

I drop my forehead to hers and stare deep into her lovely blue eyes. "I have wished many times that I were human, Halla. If I were, I would ask you to be mine, and if you accepted me, I would never let you go. I love you, Halla, but I do not expect you to return my affection." I close my eyes against the pain. "Please, I cannot bear to think of you accepting another man, especially one who does not deserve you."

She touches my cheek. "You love me?"

I stare deep into her luminous blue eyes. "More than anything, Halla. I wish so desperately that I were human."

She leans in and brushes her lips against mine in a featherlight touch. I draw in a shaking breath as she whispers against them, "It doesn't matter to me if you are Mer and I am human. I love you too, Errik."

I pull her into my arms and run my hand through her long, red hair, gripping the silken strands between my fingers. I tip her head up and capture her mouth in a claiming kiss.

CHAPTER 17

HALLA

Errik claims my mouth in a passionate kiss that steals the breath from my lungs. His lips taste like ocean and sunlight.

He wraps his arms around me and rolls me beneath him. I'm wearing only my silken undergarments. He traces his hand down my bare form and cups my breast.

I moan as he brushes the pad of his thumb over the peak. He moves down my body and grips the hem of my bra, pulling it down to free my breasts. He closes his mouth over the already stiff peak of my left breast and rubs his palm over the other. He is careful of his claws as he touches me.

The soft scrape of his teeth across my nipple makes me gasp, sending ripples of pleasure straight to my core. I thread my fingers through his hair, holding him in place.

His powerful form is made of thick layers of muscle, and I love the weight of his body over mine.

I do not have full sensation in my lower body, but I feel enough to register something hard, warm, and slick across my inner thigh. I gasp when it presses between my folds, and I realize it is his manhood. Only the thin fabric of my underwear separates us.

He pulls back sharply. "Forgive me," he breathes. "I—"

I grip the back of his neck and pull his lips back down to mine. "It's all right. I want you, Errik."

He crushes his lips to mine and rolls his hips against me. The delicious, warm heat of his length rests between us. I reach down to wrap my hands around him, surprised that he is so large, my fingers do not quite reach. His length is textured with several small bumps of flesh that secrete some sort of clear viscous fluid, making him feel slick against my palm.

I glance down to study him. Althea told me about human men, and I do not believe they look like this.

He brushes the hair back from my face. "You find my stav strange." I hear the concerned question in his tone.

"No," I breathe. "Just different. But not in a bad way, Errik."

He grits his teeth as I gently stroke his length.

He trails his hand up my inner thigh. He pulls my underwear to one side then drags his fingers through my already slick folds.

I moan when they brush over the hooded pearl of flesh at the top. Encouraged by my response, he continues to tease his thumb over my sensitive flesh and gently inserts one finger into my core. At first, the pressure feels tight and uncomfortable, and my body needs a moment to relax. Once I do, he inserts another finger, gently pumping into me.

I've touched myself before, but it's never felt like this. Every nerve is hypersensitive.

I continue to stroke his stav. His length presses against my inner thigh. He is so close to where I want him, but I don't want him to stop what he's doing. It feels amazing.

A spark of heat flares inside me as pleasure coils tightly in my core. I'm so close to the edge, and I think he is, too. His stav grows even slicker in my grasp.

"Errik," I barely manage to breathe through my pleasure. "Please."

I'm not even sure what I'm asking for, but he begins to quicken the pace of his fingers inside me. Every muscle in my body tenses, and then I'm coming harder than I ever have as pleasure roars like fire through my veins.

I cry out his name. His stav pulses in my hand and against my thigh as he comes, warm fluid erupting onto my body for what seems like forever. When I look down, my skin is covered in his essence, the blue fluid warm and sticky.

He moves to one side, pulling me with him. His stav is still a hard bar between us. It seems what Althea told me about human men needing time to recover after their climax does not apply to the Mer.

Errik's blue eyes study me as we lie in each other's arms. Illumination in the corner of my eye catches my attention, and I look down. "Your tail, Errik. It's glowing."

His mouth drifts open. The blue light is beautiful against his matching scales. "I was right," he breathes.

"What do you mean?"

"Mer tails only glow when we find our fated mates." He lifts his gaze to me and smiles. "You are mine, Halla. Fate led us to each other. I knew it deep in my soul." He captures my mouth in a claiming kiss. When he pulls back, he drops his forehead gently to my own and runs his fingers through my long scarlet hair. "You are my fated one. I long to bind you to me, Halla, and claim you as my mate."

I want more than anything to be his, but I'm just a bit nervous.

Sensing my hesitation, he cups my chin, tipping my face up to his. "What is wrong?"

"It's just… I've never done this before. I've heard making love can be painful the first time."

He presses a tender kiss to my lips. "We do not have to do anything you do not wish. You love me. That is enough, Halla. I would never ask you for anything you would not give."

I nestle into his embrace and after a while, I drift off to sleep in his arms.

CHAPTER 18

ERRIK

As she lies sleeping in my arms, myriad thoughts flit through my mind. I must give her my kiss and take her to my father. Surely, he will accept her when he finds out she is my fated one.

I must go to him as soon as possible. He is still praying that I will agree to a betrothal with Luriel, so I must quickly dispel him of this false hope. Now that I have found my fated one, he cannot argue against my reasoning.

If he refuses to give me his blessing, so be it. I will not give up Halla.

As I hold her to my chest, I am already imagining our future. I've never been happier. However, as the sun begins to set, casting long streaks of pale orange and gold across the water, I know she must return to the castle. It is only a matter of time before her brother starts looking for her, and I do not believe she wants to be discovered like this.

My gaze travels down her form. I cannot contain the

fierce possessiveness that fills me as she snuggles even closer. My nostrils flare, as I breathe deeply of our combined scent. She is mine. It matters not what my father says. I will not give her up.

CHAPTER 19

HALLA

"Halla?" Errik's voice is low in my ear. "You must wake up."

My eyes snap open, and I stretch my body against him. He wraps his arms tighter around me and presses a tender kiss to my lips. "There are things I must do," he whispers softly. "But I will meet you back here again tomorrow, my beautiful Halla."

I love the way he calls me his. "If I am yours,"—I reach up and touch his cheek—"then you are mine."

His glowing blue eyes study me as he cups my chin and gently brushes his thumb across my lips. "I have always been yours, Halla."

When he takes me back to shore, I quickly pull my dress back on, and he helps me back into my chair. Gripping the handrails, he lifts himself and seals his mouth to mine in a tender kiss full of promise.

I watch him leave before I start up the ramp for the castle. I'm almost to the top when I hear someone calling out for Errik.

I return to shore and immediately recognize his brother. As soon as he sees me, he swims toward me. I'm struck again by how similar he is to Errik. I would know they were brothers even if I'd never met him before.

"Errik just left a few minutes ago."

Another Mer swims up beside Toren. His glowing green eyes widen slightly as they meet mine before narrowing. "Who is—"

"This is Princess Halla," Toren tells him. "She is a… friend of Errik's. Halla,"—he gestures to the Merman—"this is Haldran."

His expression softens. "It is an honor to meet you, Princess."

I give him a polite smile. "And you as well."

Toren turns to him. "She said that Errik just left recently."

Haldran dips his chin in a subtle bow. "This is good news, my Prince. Perhaps he is already on his way back to your father. We should return as well, then. The King wanted to announce the royal engagement as soon as possible."

"Royal engagement?" I ask, confused.

"Yes," Haldran smiles. "It is glorious news. Prince Errik is to bond with Princess Luriel of Itlana."

I blink at him. "Errik is engaged?"

Toren's eyes meet mine, concern evident behind them. "It is not official yet and he has not agreed to—"

"He never even told me he was a prince." Pain settles deep in my chest, and I feel as if I can barely breathe. "He lied to me."

"Halla, he—"

"It's all right, Toren." I struggle to keep my voice even. "I'm glad I found out. It's better that I know. Thank you for telling me."

Devastation fills me, but I force myself to blink back my tears as I start back to the castle.

"Halla, wait!" Toren calls out, but I keep going, afraid that if I turn back I'll be unable to hold in my despair.

My pain is too raw right now, and I don't want to cry in front of him. Anger wars with sadness. I thought Errik loved me as I love him, but I was wrong.

As I make my way back up the ramp to the castle, I'm surprised to find King Henrick waiting for me in a courtyard. I quickly brush away the tears on my cheeks. "King Henrick, I did not expect to see you this early."

His expression is grim. "You're in love with a Merman."

I cast about for a suitable reply before I realize that this man does not mince words. He is as blunt as he is honest, so I decide I will be the same. "I thought I was, but—"

"I overheard. He is engaged, and judging by the tears in your eyes, it was a shock to you. Am I correct?"

Gritting my teeth, I nod.

He studies me with a piercing blue gaze and an expression I cannot quite discern. After a moment, he steps closer. "Then what is holding you here? Why not marry me and let me take you far from this place? The Mer do not stray as far north as Arnafell, and you won't have to ever see him again."

My brow furrows. "It does not bother you that I—"

He shakes his head. "No. As long as you pledge to be faithful to me after we're wed, I'll not hold any prior lovers against you." He takes my hand. "I am truly looking for an intelligent woman to be by my side and give me heirs. I will be faithful to you and give you whatever you want. I'm only asking you to rule Arnafell with me and help me raise our family. I do not expect to win your heart, only your hand and your pledge to remain at my side."

I open my mouth to speak, but he continues unencumbered.

"You are beautiful, and it is easy to see you are possessed of great intelligence. I do not care if you're broken. I still want you as my wife and future queen if you will give me your hand."

This man is impossible. He speaks the truth, no matter how blunt. However, I suppose that is an asset here. I can believe he is truly not angry and likely will not hold my rejection against me.

"I appreciate your honesty, even if it is hard to hear some of the words that leave your mouth."

For the first time since I've met him, his lips tip up in a faint smile. "Aye, I've been told that many times. I cannot help it; I was raised this way."

I arch a brow. "I believe I am beginning to understand that." I clear my throat. "However… love is important to me, Henrick. I do not think I can live my life without it, to be honest."

He studies me for a moment. "So that is a refusal, then, of my offer?"

"I believe it must be," I reply.

He draws in a deep breath and takes my hand again. "If you change your mind, my offer will still stand."

He starts to walk away but stops. Slowly, he turns back to face me with a question. "Are you not going to ask me to lend aid to your kingdom?"

I shake my head. "You made it very clear that you would only help if I agreed to marry you."

He smiles. "You see? That's why I like you. We are the same. You do not play games nor try to manipulate others."

His lips quirk up in another rare smile. "I will help your kingdom anyway."

My head jerks back. "You will?"

"Aye. Who knows? Maybe you'll look favorably upon me and decide you want me after all." He shrugs. "Or perhaps it will just lead to better trade relations between us. Either way, despite my bad manners, I am not cold of heart. I would not let others suffer when I could easily offer my help."

My mouth drifts open. I misjudged this man. He is kind... in a strange way.

He grins again. "I have brought a smile to your face. I can see I've surprised you, but pleasantly. Am I correct?"

I laugh. "Yes, you are, King Henrick."

"Just call me Henrick."

"Henrick," I repeat. "Shall we go give my brother the good news?"

"Aye. Lead the way." He gestures to the door. "If you change your mind and decide you want me, tell me before we reach him because I'd need to officially ask for your hand."

"I'm sorry, Henrick, but there is little chance of that."

He laughs. "Still, a man has to try, does he not?"

I laugh with him. "I suppose he does."

CHAPTER 20

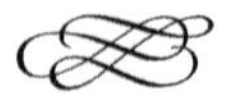

ERRIK

I have to tell Father about Halla. But before I do that, I must speak with Princess Luriel. She deserves to hear the truth before anyone else. She has been nothing but kind to me, and I do not wish to slight her by having her hear my news from someone else first.

When I reach the palace, I head straight to the guest wing. When I reach her door, I lift my hand to knock, but it opens right away, and I find her standing on the other side.

Her lavender eyes widen in surprise. *"Prince Errik,"* she says. *"I—I was just going to look for you."*

"You were?"

She nods. *"I'd like to speak with you a moment."*

"Of course."

She motions for me to follow her out into the gardens. The rows of seaweed sway gently back and forth in the current. Their white flowers are a lovely contrast to the pink coral that surrounds them. I watch as a school of brightly colored fish weave in and out of their stalks.

"It's beautiful here," she says.

I swim up beside her, allowing my gaze to travel over the city below. The castle sits up on a high shelf, overlooking its splendor, as Mer and fish swim past, going about their day. It is rare that I ever stop to truly appreciate the view. *"Yes, it is,"* I agree. *"Itlana is stunning as well."*

She nods and turns to me. *"There is something I must tell you."*

"I must speak with you as well," I add.

"You first," she says, and I notice the way she clasps her hands tightly in front of her as if worried.

"I... cannot bond with you, Luriel. I am in love with another."

She blinks and then a wide smile curves her mouth as her shoulders sag forward in relief. *"Oh, thank the god of the sea,"* she sighs. *"I am as well."*

"You are?" I grin.

"Yes. I did not know how to tell you, or how to even tell my father."

"I am the same," I admit.

She shakes her head. *"My father wants this union between us desperately. He believes we need it to secure the peace between our two kingdoms, but I think we can still have an alliance without it."*

"I do as well," I tell her.

I hold out my arm and she takes it, clasping her hand around my forearm as I do the same to hers. *"As the heir to the throne of Atena, I vow to keep the alliance and peace between us."*

She smiles. *"And I promise the same."*

I'm nervous as we go to speak with our fathers, worried that mine will ask *who* the fortunate mermaid is that I am in love with.

When we reach the throne room, both of them turn toward us expectantly. My father's smile falters when his gaze meets mine. Something in my expression must tell him that what I have to say will not be the good news he was hoping for.

I open my mouth to speak, but Luriel beats me to it.

"Father," she says. *"Errik and I have decided not to bond."*

His jaw drops, but he quickly snaps it shut. He turns a worried gaze toward my father who is leveling an icy glare at me.

My father straightens. *"What is the meaning of this, Errik?"*

"Luriel and I are not in love. We cannot bond with each other."

"Of course, you are not in love. It is too early for that yet." He places a hand on my shoulder. *"You must give it time."*

I exchange a worried glance with Luriel, and then turn my attention back to him. *"We are each in love with other people,"* I explain. *"That is why we cannot bond."*

Her father gasps. *"Is this true?"*

"Yes, Father," she replies. *"It is."*

He embraces her warmly. *"Why did you not say anything? I would never force you to marry someone you do not want."*

I arch a brow at my father, and he purses his lips.

Luriel's father turns to mine. *"Let us continue with the negotiations of a permanent alliance. The Kingdom of Itlana does not require a bonding to secure our treaty. What say you?"*

He reaches for my father and they each clasp each other's forearms. *"Agreed,"* my father replies.

My shoulders sag forward in relief.

"Errik!" my brother calls out in my mind, and I realize he must be nearby.

"Excuse me," I bow to them.

"Of course," Luriel's father says even as mine narrows his eyes at me.

I rush out into the hallway and find Toren swimming toward me so fast, it worries me. *"What is wrong?"*

"You did not tell Halla about Luriel or your birthright?"

Panic stills my heart, followed swiftly by anger. *"What did you do?"*

"You're angry with me?" he asks incredulously. *"You are the one keeping secrets. From both your family and the human you've been spending so much time with. How could you not tell her you were to be engaged?"*

"Because Luriel and I have agreed to not bond with each other. So, I'm not engaged, that's why!"

He tips up his chin. *"Then you need to tell Father."*

Devastation wars with anger as I study my brother. It is bad enough that I hadn't yet told Halla I was the prince—now she believes I'm betrothed, too. *"I did. Just now, in fact."*

"You did?"

"Yes."

"And... he was not angry?"

"I do not have time to answer your questions," I snap. *"I have to undo the damage you've done. I have to find Halla."*

"Why?"

"Because I love her, Toren!" I gesture to my tail, the faint glow barely visible at the mention of her name, but still there. It will only glow brighter once I'm near her again. *"She is my fated one. My markings began to glow last night when we—"* I stop short of telling him what we did.

His eyes widen as his face pales. *"You already mated with her?"*

"No, I have not."

His shoulders relax. *"Thank goodness. You cannot mate a human, Errik."*

"Why not?"

"I overheard your conversation with Dorin. Humans do not mate for life, so a bonding would never work between you. You would always be apart, and eventually, your relationship would suffer under the constant strain."

I do not want to hear any more. I spin to return to Solwyck.

"Where are you going?"

"To find Halla. I must explain to her. She thinks I'm betrothed, and I cannot allow her to think that I've betrayed her, Toren."

Toren swims up beside me, grasping my arm. *"Please, Brother. Do not go. You should not be with a human."*

"I love her, Toren. Don't you understand?"

"If you must go to her, fine." He releases his grip on my arm. *"But please... do not mate her. Do not bind yourself to a human."*

"I love her."

"Do you think Father and I do not love you, as well? That we do not worry for you? I don't want you to end up like that poor Mer who was left behind by his human mate when she took their child."

"Halla would not do that. She loves me, and I love her."

I do not wait for my brother to protest further. Instead, I swim as fast as I can back to the castle. I must find Halla and explain myself to her. I hate that she believes I betrayed her.

CHAPTER 21

HALLA

I'm devastated, but I push down my emotions as Henrick and I give Gerold the good news. Henrick will help us if we need assistance, which I suppose we will since I am likely never to see Errik again.

He offered us treasure from the sea, but I won't hold him to that promise, and I doubt I could bear to speak to him or even see his face now. Not after his betrayal.

Especially not after what happened between us.

Before Henrick leaves, he drops to one knee before me. "If I offended you, know that I meant none. I simply know no other way to express myself."

I smile. "I see that now, Henrick. I'm glad we understand one another."

He nods. "If you change your mind, I think you'd make a fine mother to our cubs."

"Cubs?" I blink, confused.

"Did I not tell you?" he smiles. "I'm a polar bear shifter."

Gerold and I exchange a look, and my brother's expression tells me this is news to him, as well.

Henrick bows to me then nods at Gerold. "I'll have my men unload the trunks that were meant to buy your hand. You have warranted my help for free, it seems."

Gerold bows as well. "Thank you, King Henrick."

"My people will be upset that I've returned without a mate but happy we have gained some friends and allies."

With that, King Henrick leaves. Gerold turns to me then motions to the door. "Are you sure you do not want him? He turned out to be a rather decent fellow after all."

"Yes, but he would not love me." I sigh. "At least... not in the way I want to be loved."

Gerold nods. "I believe you are right. You would have devotion, care, and faithfulness, but probably not love." He arches a brow. "Though I must admit, now that I know what he is, I would have had some interesting nieces and nephews to look forward to if you two had married."

I laugh for a moment before my expression sobers as my thoughts turn to Errik.

"What is wrong, my dear sister?"

I lift my gaze to Gerold and see the worry in his eyes. We've always been close, and he is skilled at reading me. I do not want to lie to him when I've already kept secrets for weeks now. "There is something I must tell you."

"What is it?"

"I was... in love with someone. And—" My breath hitches. "I found out that he lied to me, Gerold. He said he loved me, too, but he already belonged to someone else."

My brother turns a murderous gaze toward the doors. "Who is it? One of the guards?"

I stop short of rolling my eyes. Of course, he would suspect them first. Who else have I been around that he knows of? I can only imagine him questioning the poor men if I do not tell him everything now. "No, it was not one of the guards."

His expression morphs into confusion. "Well, who then? Certainly not Henrick."

I shake my head even as the first tear drips from my lashes.

Althea appears in the doorway. "It was the Merman, wasn't it?"

My eyes snap up to her. "How did you know?"

"The Merman that rescued you?" Gerold's wide eyes shift to Althea then narrow.

She approaches and takes my hand. "I tried to shield you from him, my dear. The day I found you on the beach after the dragon attack, I lied. I saw him with you and knew you remembered him in your dreams, but I did not want to tell you."

"Why?"

"Yes," Gerold growls. "Why would you keep secrets from us, Althea?"

Her eyes brighten with tears. "Because I wanted to spare you the pain my parents suffered, Halla. You do not know how terrible it is to be a child of two worlds."

I don't understand. "What do you mean, Althea?"

She lowers her head, and a tear slips down her cheek. She quickly brushes it away as she turns her green eyes to us both. "My father was a Merman, and my mother was human."

We gasp in unison.

"My mother grew tired of living separate lives. She fell out of love with my father and took me away when I was only seven years old." A broken sob shakes her. "I loved my father and missed him so much, but she insisted we never see him again. It was"—her voice hitches—"terrible, and I wanted to spare you that, Halla. To keep you from having a child with a man who can never share your world, just as you can never truly share his. If a child were born of your union, you could lose them as well if it was born with a Mer tail instead of human legs."

Gerold and I stare in stunned silence. I had no idea about Althea's parentage.

She squeezes my hand. "Please, Halla, do not give your heart to him. One of you will break eventually. That is the only future a Mer and a human can have: despair and heartbreak." Her voice quavers. "It cost my father his life."

I tug her into an embrace. "I'm sorry that happened to you, Althea, but you don't have to protect me. I… found out that he does not truly love me after all. He is already betrothed to another." I wipe the tears from my face. "So, you do not have to worry about me. I'm done with the sea and her Mer."

Out of the corner of my eye, I notice Gerold gaping. "When were you planning to tell me you were in love with Merman?"

I sigh heavily. "Oh, Gerold. Do not be angry with me; I cannot bear it today, my dear brother. My heart is broken, and I—"

He walks over to me and embraces me warmly. He pulls Althea into the hug as well, just like we used to embrace when we were children.

"Of course, I'm not angry with you. You know I never could be. I love you both." He levels a stern gaze at us. "But no more secrets. All right?"

Althea and I nod.

~

As Gerold takes me back to my room, I fight back my miserable tears. I refuse to break down in front of my brother or anyone else.

When the doors close behind him, I change into my nightdress. I sit in my chair and wheel myself onto the balcony, staring up at the stars. Tears spring to my eyes unbidden even as I try to push my sadness down.

I don't want to cry over Errik—not after he betrayed me—but I cannot help it. My heart is broken, and I fear it will never be whole again. How could I allow myself to fall in love with a Mer? It never would have worked.

He must have believed the same, or he wouldn't have professed to love me while betrothed to a Mermaid. I cross my arms over my chest. Maybe he did love me… just not enough. Not as much as I loved him.

I would have given him everything. My body, mind, heart, and soul. Althea was right to try to keep me from him. Even knowing what happened to her parents, I still would have taken a chance and chosen Errik—if he had wanted me. That's how much I loved him.

I lift my gaze to the moon as sobs wrack my body. I love him still.

CHAPTER 22

ERRIK

I race back to Solwyck, desperate to find Halla and explain. I can hardly bear knowing that she believes I betrayed her and that I am engaged to another after giving my heart to her.

When I reach the shoreline, I survey the castle. A light burns on her balcony, so I call out her name. "Halla!"

She does not answer.

I try again, but the strong wind swallows the sound of my voice. It is futile. She will never hear me from down here.

Not for the first time, I curse that I am not human. If I were, I could easily make my way to her, but my tail complicates everything. It does me no good at all on land because it is so cumbersome.

I swim close to the cliff wall. The tide is high and has swallowed the shoreline until no beach remains between the sea and the wall. I gauge that the climb to her balcony would be difficult but not impossible. My people are possessed of great strength.

The rock wall is jagged but has plenty of handholds I can grasp. Drawing in a deep breath, I grip the rock tightly and begin to ascend. The climb is not an easy one. Each handhold is slick and shallow, and my lower half is completely useless as I scale the wall. However, I refuse to give up. I need to speak with her and let her know I am not betrothed. My heart belongs only to her.

After what feels like forever, I manage to reach the shallow ledge beneath her balcony window. When I glance down at the water, I swallow thickly as I realize just how high I've climbed.

I close my eyes, my nostrils flaring to detect her delicate scent on the breeze. I listen carefully, training my ears for any noise she might make, but the roar of the sea is so loud I can hear nothing.

"Halla?" I call then wince, worried one of the guards might overhear.

When she doesn't respond, I try again. This time, I hear her answer. "Errik?"

"Yes!"

"Go away." Her voice trembles. "I don't want to speak to you."

"Please, Halla. I've climbed all this way because I need to—"

"Where are you?" Alarm creeps into her tone.

When I crane my neck, I notice her long, red hair swaying back and forth in the ocean breeze near the balcony railing. She peers into the darkness as if searching for me.

"I'm below you. On the ledge," I mutter, taking care not to startle her.

She looks over the edge and gasps. "Are you mad? If you fall, it will be to your death!"

I smile because her concern means she still cares for me.

All hope is not lost. "I would rather risk death than allow you to falsely believe that I do not love you."

"I trusted you, Errik." Her voice trembles and breaks. "Your brother told me about your engagement. I loved you, and you betrayed me."

"I am not betrothed. My father wants me to marry Princess Luriel, and I've refused. I already told her about you. My father was holding out false hope that I would eventually agree to bond with her—to keep the alliance between our kingdoms. Where my father is concerned, it is sometimes easier to just ignore him than to argue. He took my silence as assent when it was not." I pause. "I do not want anyone but you, Halla."

Her brow furrows. "Toren said you're a prince. Heir to the throne. All this time, you never told me. Why?"

"Because I wanted to know you as simply Errik, nothing else. I hoped you would love me for who I am instead of my title. I'm sorry, Halla."

"How can you claim to love me when you kept so many secrets from me?"

"I was a fool. Please, forgive me. I cannot bear to live without you."

Her silence worries me. After a moment, she finally speaks. "You will have to learn to live without me, Errik." Panic tightens my chest. "We can never truly be together. We are too different. I realize this now."

"We can be, Halla—you said so yourself. You said it did not matter that you are human and I am Mer. You live by the sea. We will always be near each other—"

"*Near* each other," she repeats soberly, sadness plain on her face, "but never truly together, Errik. I can see that clearly now." She pauses. "Did you know we could have conceived a child? If we had—"

"I have heard this," I reluctantly admit. "It is why I did not bind you to me last night on the rocks. I have heard that children born of mixed unions are either Mer or human. I… did not want to risk conceiving a child without—"

"Telling me first? Yet another thing you concealed from me." She pulls back from the balcony until I can no longer see her. "Henrick may have been blunt, but he, at least, spoke the truth."

Jealousy pours in like bitter acid at the mention of his name. "His ship is still docked. Do you mean to bind yourself to him now?"

"No, Errik. He gave me the truth: he could offer everything but love. Ironically, I believed *you* could offer me that. Little did I know I would have to surrender honesty; it seems you cannot offer both. At least… not to me."

Her words stab my heart. "Please, Halla. Forgive me."

"I want to, Errik, but I—"

Alarms begin blaring from the city. I twist toward the docks, and notice people racing back and forth.

Through the fog shrouding the inky darkness, something moves. Even with my superior night vision, it is difficult to make out. I squint my eyes as if that will somehow help me to see.

At least a dozen dark-gray sails emerge from the mist, approaching the harbor.

"Who is that?" Halla asks, her voice laced with quiet fear. "What are those ships?"

Fear steals through me. Not for my safety, but for Halla and her people. I have heard tales of ships with gray sails—horrible stories of cities left in ruin, people taken forcibly and sold into slavery.

"Pirates." The word leaves my mouth before I can catch it. I climb the remaining, short distance to her balcony and pull myself over the railing.

She inhales sharply, her eyes wide. "What are you—"

"I need to get you to safety, Halla." I extend my hand. "Please, come with me before it is too late."

She shakes her head. "I cannot just abandon my brother or my people, Errik."

"Halla," I plead, desperate for her to see reason. "Listen to me. I have heard stories of these ships. I will not allow them to take you. You must come with me."

Her door bursts inward, slamming against the wall as her brother rushes in. His jaw drops when he sees me on the balcony.

"What are you doing here?" he asks, his voice thunderous.

"I came to speak with Halla. There are pirate ships in your harbor. I'm trying to convince her to flee to safety with me."

King Gerold turns to his sister. "Halla, he's right. You must go with him."

"I won't leave you, Gerold."

His eyes flicker frantically with panic and indecision before steeled resolve hardens his gaze. "You must. Our defenses cannot fight them off. Once they dock, we will be forced into a battle on land. If they breach the castle, they may kidnap you—or worse. I will not allow that to happen."

"I can fight, Gerold."

"No, Halla, you cannot. Not as you are. I'm sorry. You must go with him." His gaze shifts to me. "Before it is too late."

An explosion splits the air behind me, and I whip my head toward the harbor just as King Henrick's ship fires a cannon at the closest invading pirate vessel.

Gerold rushes to the balcony's edge. "Henrick took one down, but there are dozens." He spins back to Halla, gripping her shoulders. "Please, Halla. Go. I must know you are safe."

Her eyes swell with tears. "I do not want to leave you, Gerold. You're the only family I have left."

"You must, Halla. If I fall in battle, you are Solwyck's queen. You must live. Do you understand?" He searches her eyes. "You must live, Halla."

Another explosion sounds from the harbor. Panic tightens my chest. "We have to go, Halla. Now."

She nods and turns her attention back to Gerold, hugging him tightly. "I love you, Gerold. Please, whatever you do... you must survive, my dear brother. Please."

He drops his forehead to hers. "I will do my best. Now go."

Reluctantly, she wheels closer to me. I wrap my arm around her and peer over the balcony. I am familiar enough with this part of the sea that I know where the rocks lie below and where we must aim when we jump.

"We have to jump." I look back at her. "That is the fastest way."

Fear bleeds into her eyes as she looks over the balcony at the water below.

"You have to trust me, Halla. Please."

She nods shakily. "I do."

My heart clenches as I place her on the edge of the balcony, readying to jump. I cast one last glance at her brother, who watches us intently. "I am Prince Errik of Atena. I will gather my people," I vow. "We will do what we can to help you. I swear."

He dips his chin, then we drop over the side.

CHAPTER 23

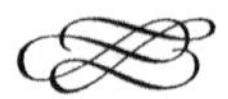

HALLA

We tumble through the air with dizzying speed. The water rises to meet us, and the world slows for a moment before we hit the surface, plunging deep into the dark waters below.

A strong current pulls at my form, ripping me from Errik's arms. I spin away, blinking in the darkness, completely disoriented and struggling to determine which way is up. My lungs burn from lack of oxygen as darkness creeps in around the edges of my vision.

Solid arms wrap around my form. Errik pulls me toward him. He seals his mouth over mine, giving me his merman's kiss. I gasp, filling my lungs with much-needed oxygen now that I'm able to breathe underwater.

He takes my hand to lead me toward our rock and to safety, but I pull back. *"Halla, we have to go,"* he speaks in my mind.

"No. We have to do something about those ships."

"We will. I will contact my people after I get you to safety."

I turn my gaze to the harbor. The ships are so close, they are almost at the docks. *"No, Errik! There isn't time. We cannot let them reach land. If we do, my brother and our soldiers will be overrun. They'll take the city and breach the castle in no time."*

He shakes his head, and I know he means to argue. Before he can protest, I tip my chin up and demand, *"Take me to the ships. We can sabotage them with the help of your people. I will not wait idly by while my people defend the city. I must do something, Errik. Please."*

Indecision plays across his face before he finally nods. He wraps his arms around me and heads toward the harbor.

He slips beneath the water, and I hear his voice in my mind as he calls to nearby Mer. *"Anyone who can hear me, this is your prince, Errik. The city of Solwyck is under attack by pirates. We must help them, or they will be overrun. Spread the word. Call all our warriors to Solwyck's harbor. We cannot allow the city to fall into the hands of pirates."*

We're halfway to the ships when his brother swims up beside us. I recognize him immediately. He speaks in my head. *"Halla, what are you—"*

"I think I know how to sabotage the ships," I interrupt.

"How?"

"Get me onto the deck of the closest one. They will have gunpowder for their cannons. If we can light it, it will destroy their ships." I face Errik. *"Spread the word among your people."*

CHAPTER 24

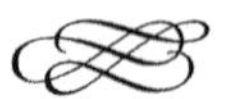

ERRIK

As soon as we reach the closest ship, Halla and I position ourselves along one side. I search for a way to pull myself up and spot a rope hanging over the edge of the deck.

Quietly, I pull myself up and reach back for Halla. Toren lifts her to me, and I haul her the rest of the way. I turn to her and whisper, "Now what?"

My gaze sweeps the deck for any sign that we've been spotted. However, all the pirates are lined up at the opposite railing, their attention focused on the city as they aim their cannons and fire in succession.

The explosions are much louder now that we're close, and I want nothing more than to cover my ears against the onslaught, but we must press on.

"We need to get that"—she points at a lantern hanging beside the door to the hold—"and throw it on those." She gestures to several barrels on deck. "It will cause the gunpowder to ignite and destroy the ship."

I lean over the edge of the deck and relay this to my brother. "Spread the word to our people. We must destroy their vessels before they dock or all may be lost."

Toren nods then slips beneath the water. Despite all the chaos that surrounds us, I notice the flash of tails in the water. My chest swells with pride. My people have answered my call and come to help the people of Solwyck once more.

"I'll get the lantern," I tell Halla.

Before she can argue, I drag myself across the deck. The coarse wood rubs against my scales. Splinters dig into my flesh, but I ignore the stinging sensation as I keep one eye trained on the pirates and the other on my goal.

When I reach the hold, the lantern is so high, I must stretch to reach it. As soon as my hand touches the handle, the door opens. My heart stops then begins hammering as I come face to face with one of the pirates.

His jaw drops, revealing a mouth missing its teeth. He releases a shaking breath, the foul stench wrinkling my nose and making my eyes swim. I take advantage of his shock and slam his head against the door. He collapses to the deck in a crumpled heap.

I gather the lantern then drop back to the wooden deck, dragging myself toward Halla.

A loud noise draws my attention, and I twist onto my back in time to see a pirate lunging at me with a knife. Unable to dodge quickly enough, I cry out when he sinks the blade deep into my side.

Blinding pain rips through me, searing my veins like fire. The pirate pulls another blade, readying to attack, but I grip the handle firmly in my side. Gritting my teeth, I pull it from my body, and plunge it deep into his chest.

I watch with cold satisfaction as the light fades from his eyes. A glance at his companions tells me no one witnessed the fight.

Blood pours from my wound, but I force myself to push past the pain. Halla needs me. I have to focus.

Quickly, I make my way back to her, wincing inwardly against the agony of each movement. Warm blood pools beneath me, my hand slipping on the red liquid by the time I reach her.

She touches my face. "How badly are you injured?"

"I'm fine," I lie, brushing off her concern. "What do we need to do with this?"

She takes the lantern from my hand. "I'm going to throw this on the powder. We must swim away as fast as we can before it explodes. All right?"

I nod. She counts to three and tosses the lantern at the barrels. The glass shatters and a fiery ball of flame bursts outward. Fire licks across the wooden planks of the deck, creeping up the barrels.

Panic constricts my chest as I grab Halla's waist and push us both over the edge of the ship, dropping into the sea. The saltwater stings my wound, but I bite back my pain as we swim away. More Mer flee with us. The screams of the pirates drown out all other sounds as they realize their ships are on fire.

"Put it out! We have to—"

A deafening *boom* splits the air, and I spin in the water, shielding Halla from the blast of heat as the ship explodes, raining down fire and debris. Another ship soon follows, exploding in a brilliant display of smoke and fire along the harbor.

My vision blurs as I struggle to stay conscious. Halla's voice barely penetrates the fog, the sound distant even though she is in my arms.

"Errik?" My brother grabs me, pulling me to him. "You're bleeding!"

Halla brushes the hair back from my face as I float limply in the water, my gaze fixed on the sky overhead.

I take her hand, squeezing with the last of my strength. "You are my heart, Halla. I love you."

Closing my eyes, I fall away into darkness.

CHAPTER 25

HALLA

Panic stops my heart. "He's losing too much blood, Toren. We have to get him to shore and staunch the bleeding."

He grabs Errik, pulling him past the burning ships to the shoreline. Mangled bodies float amidst the debris, but I push through the corpses as we make our way to the beach.

A white bear rushes across the sand. My heart stills for a beat before I realize it must be Henrick. He skids to a halt in front of us, his eyes black as his nostrils flare. "Your Merman?" he asks, and I note his voice is a rumbling growl in his bear form.

Toren watches him warily as he holds his brother's limp form in his arms.

"Can you find Healer Althea and bring her here?" I ask.

He nods his massive head and starts back toward the castle.

Other white bears lumber along the shoreline, mingling with Solwyck's humans. Henrick and his men must have been preparing to defend the harbor and the city in case the pirates docked.

In the distance, I notice a flash of red hair. "Gerold!" I cry out.

His head whips toward me, and he races down to the beach. He drops to his knees before me, gathering me into his arms. "Thank the gods you are safe." His eyes sweep to Errik, and he gasps. "What happened?"

"One of the pirates stabbed him while we were lighting fire to the ships. Errik's people—"

"Saved the city," Gerold finishes my sentence. He hugs me again. "And so did you."

Tears stream down my face as I study Errik. "We have to help him, Gerold."

I cup Errik's cheek, turning his face to me. I press a tender kiss to his lips. "Please, Errik. You have to live, my love."

Several Mer gather around us, bowing in mourning as they observe their prince.

The crowd parts to allow a Merman wearing a golden crown through. He stops on the shore beside Errik. Toren's eyes are full of tears as he addresses him. "Father, Errik's been hurt."

Another Merman approaches behind him. He rushes to Errik's side, laying his hands over his injury as he studies him. "What happened?"

"One of the pirates stabbed him while we were trying to sabotage the ship," I explain, unable to hide the quaver of my voice.

A collective gasp moves through the crowd, and I look up to find Henrick running to the shore with Althea on his back.

"It's all right," I tell the Mer. "The bear is King Henrick. He will not harm you."

Althea slides off his back and drops to her knees beside Errik, her brows drawn as she assesses his wound.

"Who are you?" the Mer already examining him asks.

"I am Healer Althea. Who are you?"

"Healer Dorin."

Together, they run their hands over him while the rest of us look on anxiously. After a moment, Althea pulls back, sorrow in her voice. "His wound is fatal."

The king levels a dark glare at her. "Who are you to make this determination?"

She tips her chin up. "I am a Healer, and I am half Mer. My father was one of your people, and my mother was human."

Dorin's face pales. "You are the child… your human mother took you away."

"Yes."

Errik's father studies her a moment, bowing his head slightly in acknowledgement before he turns his gaze back to me. "This is the human you told me about?" he addresses Toren.

"Yes, Father. Errik says she is his fated one."

Clenching his jaw, he faces me. "This is true? You love my son?"

I drop my gaze to Errik. "With all my heart." I draw in a deep and steeling breath, then lift my eyes to him again. "I am going to save him."

CHAPTER 26

HALLA

For all his massive size in his bear form, Henrick is quite nimble, even with me on his back. We pick our way through the woods toward the blood witch's cabin.

I've never ventured this deep into the forest. The trees are so densely grouped, they create a canopy overhead that the sun's rays cannot penetrate. If I did not know any better, I'd believe it was nearly dark instead of only midmorning.

Dorin and Althea believe Errik is beyond hope, that he has very little time left before he crosses from this world to the next, and that I should just give up. However, I refuse to accept his fate. Many things may seem impossible until they aren't.

Before a dragon attacked the city, I never believed I could slay one. Before I lost the ability to walk, I never thought I'd still be able to live a full life. Until I was challenged, I never knew exactly what I was capable of.

"You are certain this is the way?" Henrick asks, pulling me back from my thoughts.

"Yes." I pause. "I can never thank you enough for carrying me, Henrick. No one else would have brought me if not for you."

"My motives are not purely unselfish, you know," he replies.

I still, wondering if he will ask me to marry him again. Surely he'd realize that the answer would be no. After all, he is taking me to a blood witch to make a deal to save my Merman lover's life.

He continues, "I do this because of the great balance."

"The great balance? What is that?" I ask, curious to understand.

"All actions have consequences—good and bad. The choices we make are weighed in the grand scheme of things. Some call it fate, others chance. Whatever name you choose, the balance exists nonetheless."

"I don't understand," I admit.

"You saved your city from a dragon and lost your legs. Now you will sacrifice again to save your Merman." He pauses to allow the weight of his words to settle between us. "If the balance holds true, this will be repaid to you in kind. You will save him, and someone will eventually save you."

My brow furrows. "From what?"

He shrugs, shifting me slightly on his back. "I do not know. However, I do expect that since I've helped you, someday someone else may be inclined to offer me aid when I need it in turn."

I consider his words. "That is an interesting worldview."

He nods. "It is the way of the North."

That seems to be his answer for everything, and I find myself curious to visit Arnafell now. To see how these people of the North live with their blunt truths and manners, and yet, hearts of solid gold.

Ahead, a clearing shines brightly in the distant dark, a patch of light filtering in from above. A meager cabin sits in the center. With a thatched roof, two windows, an aged wooden door, and a compact garden to one side, one would never suspect what lies within.

As we approach, my nerves begin to fail me. I clench my hands into fists, clinging to Henrick's fur to try to still their shaking. When we reach the door, I steel myself and slide off his back.

He shifts back into his human form, and I'm surprised to see him clothed even though he explained this to me on our way here. Just as he shifts from one form to the next, he can conjure the appearance of clothing so as not to appear naked.

He lifts me into his strong arms and holds me tightly to his chest as I knock on the door.

"Enter!" A woman's voice calls from inside.

Henrick pushes the door open, and the strong scent of herbs greets us. The floor is bare earth. In one corner, a worn wooden worktable is covered in bottles of unlabeled, colorful liquids. I note all the various herbs and plants hanging from the ceiling to dry. A fireplace with a roaring fire sits along the opposite wall. Before it stands another chair, bearing a woman.

She turns, and I gape at her. She is one of the most beautiful people I've ever seen. She has long, lavender hair that hangs past her shoulders, sharp, tipped ears like the Fae or the Elves, violet skin, and amber eyes that seem to pierce me. "I have been expecting you," she says matter-of-factly.

She is a blood witch, so I do not question this statement. Besides, I am only here for one thing, and I feel we must hurry. "Then you already know what I want."

She stands and walks toward me, her eyes narrowing on

Henrick. He growls low in his throat. "Mind yourself, witch," he snarls. "I'll not allow you to hurt her."

A smirk twists her lips. "Oh, but you will if it is her choice." Her eyes shift to me, and she holds out a vial of green liquid. "This is what you have come for. Would you like to hear the price?"

As she moves closer, darkness seems to swell all around her. As if night and shadow cling to her form. She smiles and I wince inwardly when I notice two rows full of teeth, long and sharp as knives. Her nails extend into long, black claws, lethal and deadly.

I swallow against the knot of fear in my stomach. "What is the price?"

"Your love."

My head jerks back. "I don't understand."

She reaches out and runs her finger along my chin and jaw, her sharp claws grazing my skin as her amber, reptilian eyes search mine. "Many understand how powerful of an emotion love can be, but most do not realize it creates magic, as well."

"Magic?"

"Yes." Her lips curl up in a sinister grin and her sharp teeth seem to grow even longer. "One of the most powerful forms there is. You will give this potion to your Merman, and he will heal. In exchange, your memories of him, along with the love that you feel, will be transferred to me."

She caresses my face, and I jerk away from her touch as she cackles "Yes. A pure love like yours will offer me much energy indeed and help keep me beautiful and young."

Her words stop my heart. How many have made such deals with her in the past for her to appear as she does now?

I blink at her. "So, I won't remember Errik?"

"No. You will not." Her eyes shift to Henrick. "And neither

will anyone close to you. That includes you as well, Bear of the North."

My thoughts turn to my brother and Althea. If no one close to me remembers Errik and my love for him, they will not be able to remind me of what I've lost. But if Errik remembers our love, *he* can—

The Witch arches a brow. "Do you really believe that I cannot tell what you are thinking, Princess? The potion binds you. Your heart and mind will be sealed off from the man that you love. Only a magic far stronger than mine could break this enchantment. That is how it works."

Sadness stabs at my chest as she narrows her eyes at me. "Do you accept?"

A growl rumbles Henrick's chest as he addresses the witch. "She will still lose him if she takes your offer. Your price is cruel. Even *I* can see that."

"Perhaps the ice around your heart is not as thick as you believe, Bear King," A smirk twists her lips. "You believe my terms are cruel, but they are not. The Merman will live, and *you*—" she gestures to me,—"will be spared the pain that comes with love."

"What are you talking about?" I ask.

"I know a thing or two about shattered hearts, my dear. After all, it is one of the main reasons people come to me."

Henrick growls even louder.

I place a hand on his chest, and his blue eyes snap to mine. "I cannot let Errik die, Henrick. Not when I could help him."

"Good," the witch says. "Here you are." She places the vial in my hand.

Henrick's lips curl back in a feral snarl as he levels an icy glare at her. "If your potion causes any other harm to befall her, I will be your death, old woman."

She narrows her eyes. "I would expect nothing less from a King of the North."

I turn to Henrick. "Let's go. We must hurry."

~

The trip back to the city seems to take forever, but in truth, I'm sure we take less time than we took to reach the witch. Henrick knows the way back since we've already traveled it, and this knowledge lends speed to our journey.

As soon as we reach the shore, Errik's father lifts his gaze. Humans and Mer alike gather in silent vigil around Errik, who lies on a makeshift cot brought from the infirmary of the castle.

Gerold's expression is thunderous when he notices the vial. "What did you have to promise her in exchange?"

I clench my jaw and tip my chin up in determination as Henrick carries me to Errik's side. "I will lose my memories of him and forget our love for each other." I turn to Toren and take his hand as I meet his gaze evenly. I am not close to him, so I hope that his memory will not be bound by the potion's spell. "Please, tell him that I did this for him. I will not remember any of the time we have spent together."

His eyes shine with sadness as he nods grimly. "Of course."

I cup Errik's face, turning his head toward me. I lean down and press a tender kiss to his lips as a tear drips from my lashes to his cheek. "I love you, Errik."

Grief swells as I open his mouth and pour the green liquid onto his tongue. His lips move as he swallows, and darkness overwhelms me.

CHAPTER 27

ERRIK

My eyes snap open. The first thing I become aware of is my father's face leaning over me. I blink up at him. *"Father? What is going on?"*

He embraces me warmly. *"My son, thank goodness you are well again."*

I sit up, only now noticing I'm back home, in my room, instead of on the beach. *"What do you mean? I—"*

I stop as myriad pieces of memories flit through my mind. Panic tightens my chest. *"Where is Halla?"*

Pain reflects in Dorin's eyes. *"She saved you, Errik. You were near death."*

"Where is she?"

He lowers his gaze. *"They took her back to the castle. She fell unconscious after she gave you the potion."*

"Potion?" I scowl. *"What are you talking about?"*

Toren places a hand on my shoulder. *"There is much I must tell you, my dear brother."*

~

I wait along the shoreline, hoping for even one glimpse of her. It has been three weeks since she traded her love and her memory of me to save my life. Knowing that she does not remember me is a devastation unlike anything I have ever felt before.

I swallow against the lump in my throat as I observe her wheel herself to the balcony. King Henrick takes a seat beside her as they gaze out at the sea. His memory was altered as well. He is courting her, trying to convince her to become his queen.

Worry tightens my chest as I notice her spending more time with him lately. As if all this time he has spent with her these past few weeks is gently easing her into the idea of accepting his proposal.

Shortly after the potion healed my mortal wound, it imparted something else to me. I gained the knowledge of exactly what the witch took in her bargain with Halla—the details of the binding, and everyone affected.

Even if I were to try to tell Halla who I was and what I had once meant to her, she would be unable to accept it. Her heart and mind are bound by the dark magic that was used to create the potion.

Henrick is determined to make her his mate. He knows she does not love him, but he doesn't care. I overheard Halla speaking with Gerold a few weeks ago. She believed it was her duty to accept Henrick's hand because of the help he could offer her people and her kingdom in rebuilding after the dragon's attack.

My father took pity on me and met with King Gerold. He offered him several chests of treasure from the sea to help the people of Solwyck rebuild and to free Halla from the burden of having to marry a man she does not love. But more importantly, I know Father did it for me. Because he knows how devastated I am at the mere thought of her taking another as her mate.

Henrick has not given up, however. Even though her kingdom no longer needs money or aid, he offers her something she fears she may never have otherwise: children and a family of her own. She believes no one else will want her because of her disability.

If only she knew how I felt. I wish she could remember how much I love her.

As I watch her with Henrick, jealousy twists deep inside me. I want to scale the cliff wall and pull her into my arms, give her my kiss and steal her away to my palace in the depths of the sea.

I have imagined doing this many times, but I know I cannot. If I did, it would only scare her. She does not remember our love. A deep ache settles in my chest at the knowledge that she might never regain her memories of me.

A tremulous smile crests my lips as Henrick helps her to stand. Her knees shake as she steadies herself. She is unable to walk without holding onto someone for balance, but still… it is progress, and I am happy for her.

Movement ripples the water nearby, and I turn to find Toren. He swims up beside me. "You cannot keep coming here, Errik. It is not good for you. You must move on."

"She is my fated one, Toren. I love her. I cannot just forget her."

How can I ever move on knowing that the female I love is so close yet so far away?

Dorin and I have been searching for answers, and I have to believe we will find them. I have to believe this, because I refuse to give up.

Henrick takes Halla's hand and brings the back of it to his lips. A faint smile curves her mouth and bitter acid burns its way up my throat. I would set flame to his ship and happily watch it sink to the bottom of the sea if Henrick was not a good and honorable male.

But I know he is because I have listened to him speak to Halla. His words are blunt but his intentions are true. He would offer her anything and everything she could possibly want if she agrees to become his mate.

Everything but love, that is. He claims to be incapable of this emotion.

"Errik," Toren says, ripping me from my dark thoughts. "We should leave."

Sadness tears at my chest as I watch Henrick get down upon one knee on the balcony before her.

"Brother," Toren says, pulling at my arm. "We need to go. Now."

In the back of my mind, I recognize the warning in Toren's voice, but I cannot bring myself to look away from Halla.

Henrick's voice carries on the wind as he stares up at her. "Will you be my queen?"

She hesitates a moment, and my heart shatters when she finally nods, 'yes.'

"No!" the angry roar rips from my chest.

Halla's head whips toward me, but Toren drags me beneath the water.

"What were you thinking?"

Devastation wars with anger. She should be mine. Not his. *"She cannot bond with him! Henrick will never love her like I would!"*

"That is not your decision to make," Toren snaps. *"Not anymore."*

His words hit me like a physical blow.

He places a hand on my shoulder. *"Forgive me, Errik. I should not have spoken so harshly. I do not know what to say to make things better for you. You barely eat or sleep anymore. Father and I are worried; afraid that if you continue in this way, you will die of a broken heart."*

He is right. The witch may have given Halla a potion to save my life, but I am still dying slowly anyway. Numbly, I nod and allow Toren to pull me back to the castle.

As soon as we enter, Dorin appears. His eyes are full of concern as they meet mine. *"My Prince,"* he bows low. *"Please, do not despair. I believe I have found an answer to help Halla regain her memories."*

"What is it?"

"A blue pearl."

I shake my head. *"Those are a myth."*

"No," he insists. *"They are not."*

I blink at him in astonishment. *"Where can I find one? The myths mention they are extremely rare."*

"There is a dragon in Eryadon. It is rumored that he has a blue pearl; that he stole it from a Sea Witch many years ago."

"A dragon? How will I get the pearl from a dragon?"

"He is cursed and lives in a castle along the coastline. But you must be careful. He is the same dragon who burned the city of Bryndor to ash."

I still at his words. Everyone knows what happened to Bryndor. Almost the entire city was reduced to fire and ash. It still lies in ruin, even to this day. It was once the shining jewel of its kingdom, known far and wide for its beauty and as a hub of commerce and trade.

The devastation visited upon Solwyck is but a shadow of what happened there. If not for Halla's sacrifice and bravery, her city would have suffered the same fate.

"I forbid you to go on this dangerous quest," Father's voice rings in my head as he enters the room. He levels a dark glare at Dorin.

Dorin's eyes go wide and he bows low. *"Forgive me, my King. I am only trying to help."*

"By sending my son to his death?"

All the color drains from Dorin's face. *"Of—of course not, my King. I would never—"*

"And yet, you would send him to steal treasure from the Dragon that burned Bryndor to ash."

My hands curl into fists at my side as I struggle to push down my anger. *"If it were Mother, would you not do the same?"* I challenge. *"Would you not risk your life to get her back?"*

"Your mother was Mer. Halla is not. Your relationship was destined to fail from the start," he grinds out. *"Better that it happened now, before you bound yourself to her, than after."*

I gesture to my tail. The fated glow may be dim, but it is still there. *"She is my fated one. I do not want to live without her."*

"I forbid you to risk your life for a human!" Father shouts.

I tip my chin up and meet his gaze evenly. *"It is not your decision to make. It is mine."*

"Errik, you cannot—"

"That human," Toren interrupts, *"saved Errik's life. Or have you forgot?"*

Frustration burns in Father's eyes, but he says nothing. What can he say? Toren is right and the decision is mine.

I turn to Dorin. *"In the myths, it is said that the pearls only work during the blue moon cycle. Is this truth?"*

He nods. *"Once you have it, you must take it to her. Hold it in your hand and speak the words of your soul's desire. The magic of the pearl will only work if your heart is true."*

"You are certain it will work?" I ask.

He shakes his head. *"In truth, I do not know. In my research, I found that Mer used to seek out blue pearls to grant them legs so they could live among the land dwellers.*

"Blue pearls contain powerful magic, even more so than that of

a Bloodwitch. It is your best hope for breaking the curse tied to the potion. But it will only work during the blue moon cycle."

Worry fills me. There is less than a week until the blue moon comes. If I have not retrieved the blue pearl by then I will have to wait a little over two years before the next blue moon cycle. And if the dragon truly has one, who knows how long it will take me to retrieve it.

In addition to that, Henrick is now engaged to Halla. I have to restore her memories before they wed. I cannot bear the thought of her taking another as her mate.

As if reading my thoughts, Dorin places a hand on my shoulder. *"You must hurry. You do not have much time."*

With a slight clench of his jaw, Father's gaze meets mine. He pulls me into a hug. *"Know that I love you, my son, and I want only for you to be happy."*

"Then, please understand, Father. She is my heart, and I must do whatever I can to get her back. Even if it means facing down a dragon."

"I will go with you," Toren says. *"I'll help you find the blue pearl."*

Father looks to us. *"Just promise me that you will both return to me safely."*

We each give him a solemn nod. Despite my fear, I will not waver in my resolve. I will do whatever it takes to restore Halla's memories. I will retrieve the blue pearl or die trying.

CHAPTER 28

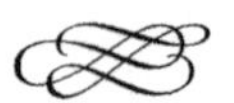

ERRIK

We have traveled down Eryadon's coastline for three long days, but I believe I have found the dragon's castle. My brother Toren swims beside me, and although I initially tried to dissuade him, I am glad for his company.

"There is a human woman with him in the castle."

My brow furrows. "Does she know who he is?"

"I do not believe so. When I went hunting yesterday, I saw them sitting on the cliff wall above the ocean. I tried luring her away to safety with my song, but it did not work."

I frown. "She must not realize he is a dragon. I will certainly inform her. Perhaps she can tell me where he keeps the pearl."

"How do you propose to get it?" Toren asks incredulously.

"It's not as if I cannot drag myself onto land." I shrug. "Yes, it will be difficult, but not impossible."

He purses his lips. "This does not seem like much of a plan."

"I know, but we have no other choice. This is the only way I can restore Halla's memories."

His gaze holds mine for a moment but he does not protest further. He knows I am right. "I will go hunting again while you keep watch."

I glance at him as he swims off, then turn my attention back to the castle. The dragon seems to split his time between the palace and a cave further down the coast. He flew off not long ago, but I will wait a few more minutes to see if he returns. I suppose I will have no choice but to just ask him for the pearl. I will give him whatever he wants in return, although I've never known dragons to want for anything.

They do love treasure and wealth, however, so I plan to offer him whatever riches I can find at the bottom of the sea. Hopefully, he will consider this a fair exchange. If he doesn't, I will simply have to steal the pearl from him somehow.

My thoughts go round in a circle as I consider my options, which are not many. In the end, I have no choice.

If I want Halla back, this is the only way, according to Dorin. I always believed the blue pearls were nothing more than a myth, but it seems I was wrong.

I only know one thing for certain: I must retrieve the blue pearl and bring it to Halla during the blue moon cycle, which is fast approaching.

The pearls are rumored to grant a wish of the wearer—their heart's greatest desire—but only if their intentions are true.

As I survey the cliff wall leading toward the dragon's castle, I notice the human woman approach. She carries a long stick that sweeps before her, every so often tapping the ground. Her long, blond hair blows around her face with the ocean breeze, and her gaze appears fixed on nothing. Her behavior is strange, and I wonder if perhaps she cannot see.

I open my mouth and begin singing, hoping to lure her to the sea. She does not know how much danger she is in with the dragon. Surely she does not, else she would not stay with him... unless she is his prisoner.

"Hello?" she calls out to me, and I stop singing.

My heart hammers as I respond, "Come down to the ocean, dear human."

"If you are one of the Mer, I have no desire to be lured into the sea," she replies. "I simply need help finding my way."

"You do not feel a pull to the ocean?" I ask, unable to hide the curiosity in my tone. I'd always heard our song could draw a human to the ocean, unless they were already in love with another.

"No. I am trying to find the dragon's cave. Surely you know where it is, for I heard your song not long ago near the cliffs."

I frown. "I will not help you find your death."

Her mouth drifts open. "Is that not what your siren call is meant to do? Lure me to the water so that I may drown?"

"No," I scoff. Does she think I am evil? "Contrary to the tales you may have heard, my kind does not lure innocents to the sea only to drown them."

"Then, why do you sing?"

"Many Mermen want a wife. Humans are rumored to be excellent lovers," I tease, trying to put her at ease. "Passionate creatures like ourselves."

When she doesn't rise to the bait, my expression sobers. "I have watched you with the dragon. I want only to save you from him. Do you know who he truly is, my lady?"

"Yes. He is the dragon who burned the city of Bryndor."

Good. She knows, so the rest should be easy. "Then you understand why I wish to lure you from his claws."

"You misunderstand," she says. "He has changed. He is not the same dragon he was before. I… I love him."

I chuckle softly. "So that is why my brother's song did not influence you. He wondered about that."

"Please, I must find the dragon before it is too late."

"Too late for what?"

"He is under a curse. I am bound to it as well. I will die at the end of the blood moon cycle if it is not broken. I must find him before then."

"So, it is true. A curse lies upon the dragon and his castle," I muse. "My people had heard of this but were uncertain."

"What is your name?" she asks.

"Errik. What is yours?"

"Alara. Will you help me to find the dragon's cave, Errik?"

I do not want to help her find the dragon, but I need the pearl. If she claims the dragon is a good man, I have no other choice but to trust her judgment. I must find the blue pearl. "If that is what you truly wish."

"I do."

"You are close. Simply continue along the cliffs, and I will stay nearby until you reach the cave."

She smiles, and my heart fills with guilt. "Thank you, Errik."

"Do not thank me," I reply somberly. "Helping you find him goes against my every instinct."

She cocks her head to the side. "Then why do you help me?"

I am compelled to admit the truth to her; Toren and I have been observing them both for the past few days. "Because I believe he cares for you… although I did not know dragons were capable of caring for another," I murmur. "I heard him call on the blood witch a few days ago. He offered his blood to the sea to get her attention, then begged her to spare his beloved. Since my song did not tempt you, I assume he was referring to you. You are obviously in love with him, as well. If you were not, my siren's song would have called you to the sea."

A smile crests her lips.

"Have you heard of what happened in Solwyck?" I ask, referring to the damage wrought by the dragon there. Solwyck would have been reduced to ash just like Bryndor if Halla had not slain the dragon.

She nods.

"Then you know that dragons are dangerous creatures."

"I know, Errik. But Veron is different."

"I hope you are right," I tell her. "You are nearly there."

"Why have you been watching Veron?"

"In truth, I seek something he owns. I was told that the dragon who lives in the kingdom of Eryadon near the sea has what I need."

"What is it?"

"I am uncertain," I answer truthfully, because I have never seen a blue pearl before; I only know that I must find one. "I was told that I would know it when I see it."

"Why do you need it?"

"It is… for a friend," I hedge, uncertain of how much to share with her. If I tell her it is for my fated mate, and she reveals this to the dragon, he will know he can demand anything in exchange. While I would not mind giving him whatever he wants, I must return to Halla as soon as possible. I do not have time to mine the ocean floor for untold amounts of lost treasure.

Instead of explaining my reasons, I change the subject. Alara and I chat as I guide her to the dragon's cave. When she draws closer, I instruct her to take only a few more paces to her right.

She turns to thank me, and I gasp when my eyes alight on

the blue pearl necklace she wears. "That necklace. Where did you get it?"

She wraps her hand around the pearl, clutching it to her chest. "Veron gave it to me."

"Please," I beg, desperate now that I've found what I'm after. "May I have it?"

"I..." She hesitates.

"Please. I need it for Princess Halla."

She blinks several times. "The Princess of Solwyck?"

"Yes."

"Alright," she agrees and begins to unfasten the clasp from around her neck.

The dragon approaches behind her in his two-legged form, glaring at me thunderously. Tall and broad-shouldered, he is covered in silver scales that gleam beneath the sun like heavy armor. His proud, dark horns spiral from his head, making him appear even taller as he stands behind her and places his hands on her shoulders. His green eyes narrow.

She traces her hands up his arms and smiles. "Veron?"

He wraps his arms around her, pulling her close. "What are you doing here?" he asks her. "Why have you come?"

I'm surprised by the tenderness in his tone and gaze as he regards her.

"I needed to find you. I—"

"Did you walk all this way by yourself?" he asks, a hint of anger shifting into his tone as he chastises her for not being careful.

She snaps back, and I note in astonishment that he looks chagrined. A human chastising a dragon? This is not something I ever thought I'd see.

She gestures to the sea. "I had help from Errik."

"A Merman?" he grinds out, leveling another dark glare at me. "The Mer are dangerous."

She places her hands on her hips. "Well, he said the same thing about dragons. If not for him, I would have been lost. I probably would have missed your cave entirely, Veron."

He bares his fangs at me, obviously displeased by her words. His gaze drops to her neck. "What are you doing with your necklace?"

"Errik said he needs it for Princess Halla of Solwyck."

"Why does the princess need this?" Veron roars at me.

"She made a deal with a blood witch," I call out. "I am trying to free her from the consequences."

Surely he understands this since I observed him summoning a blood witch a few days ago. It seems he is indebted and under a curse from one, as well.

He grows silent.

Alara takes his hand. "If it will help the princess, we should give it to him, Veron."

He lifts the necklace and pendant from her palm. "It is… an invaluable treasure from the very heart of the sea. Powerful and—"

"I don't need any treasures," she says, stroking his cheek. "All I need is you."

It does not escape me how he closes his eyes and leans into her hand as if relishing her touch.

A dragon in love with a human? I only pray that he is worthy of such love and devotion.

"Treat her well, Dragon," I interject, feeling oddly protective of this human. She reminds me of my beloved Halla. "Or you will know the wrath of the seas."

"She is mine," he growls. "I would never harm my greatest treasure." With that, he throws the pearl at me. "Take the necklace and leave us, you troublesome fish."

I leap from the water to catch it, smiling once I feel the pearl in hand. "Thank you. I will tell the princess that you helped her."

"I doubt she'll want to know that a dragon aided her," he mumbles.

"I meant Alara, not you." I laugh. "The princess has no love of dragons, as you well know. Goodbye, Alara! And thank you!"

"Goodbye, Errik!"

I race back to find my brother, anxious to return to Halla.

CHAPTER 29

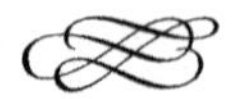

HALLA

I *dream of a man with eyes as blue as the northern sea. His hair is the color of the obsidian stone cliffs along the shoreline. As I lay on the beach, he leans over me, his gaze studying mine with an intense look of love and devotion.*

He reaches down and gently strokes my cheek. "You are my heart, Halla," he whispers. "And I am yours."

I awaken with a start. The fog of my dreams recedes. The images retreat like tides from the shore, but one thing remains—my desire to find this man.

I reach up and place my hand over my heart as if that will somehow help dull the ache in my chest. Although it is only a dream, it always feels so real.

But when I close my eyes, I can still hear his deep voice and feel the whisper of his touch across my skin. *"You are my heart, Halla. Fate led us to each other."*

I sit up in bed and grab my legs, pulling them over the edge of the bed. Carefully, I stand, mindful that I have my balance before I slowly make my way out to the balcony, overlooking the sea.

I can walk for short distances, but it is difficult. I still have not regained the full use of my legs, and more days than not, I am bound to my chair when my pain becomes too great.

I wish I could walk normally, as I used to. I remember the joy of running along the beach and then diving into the water for a swim to cool myself after. It has been so long since I swam. Perhaps I've avoided it for fear that I am not strong enough to navigate the current without the full use of my legs. But part of me suspects it is that I worry it will not be the same.

I watch as the blue moon slowly rises over the sea. It is full this night, casting shimmering reflections among the rolling waves. The crisp, saline breeze blows through my long, scarlet hair and I inhale deeply.

Something about the ocean calls to me. As if my soul is searching for something out among the waves. My thoughts turn to the man that haunts my dreams and the memory of his glowing blue eyes as he stares down at me.

He must be Mer. Their eyes glow as his do.

Moonlight spreads out across the ocean; its silver rays shimmering across the waves. I scan the surface. Many nights, I've noticed a pair of glowing blue eyes observing me from the sea. I know there are Mer in these waters, and I often wonder if the man in my dreams is among them.

Lowering my gaze, I push down these errant thoughts. Tomorrow, I will marry Henrick. He may not love me, but he does care about me in his own way. He has offered me a place to rule by his side and a chance at a life of my own, with children and family.

Gerold has tried to dissuade me, insisting that I should wait for love. But after Prince Edwyrd's rejection, because of my injury, I doubt I'll have any other offers. Besides... a marriage to Henrick would also mean a permanent alliance between our kingdoms, which would only benefit our people.

And yet, even as I think on all the reasons I have agreed to this marriage, my thoughts keep returning to the Merman's blue eyes. Why can I not stop thinking of him? In my mind, I know he is just a dream, but my heart insists that he's real.

I turn my gaze once more to the ocean and whisper aloud as his image surfaces in my thoughts. "If you are out there, find me."

With a heavy sigh I turn back to my room. Tomorrow, I marry Henrick beneath the light of the full blue moon. Once we are wed, I resolve to leave behind these ridiculous longings and fantasies. They are simply dreams… no more.

CHAPTER 30

ERRIK

I swim as fast as I can back to Solwyck, desperate to find Halla. The Blue moon is full this night. Its silver light spreading out across the waves in a shimmering display. I am nearly there. Absently, I reach for the necklace, closing my hand over the blue pearl that hangs around my neck as I send a silent prayer to whatever gods may be listening.

Please, let this work to restore Halla's memories of me.

Toren follows closely behind me as we approach Atena—the underwater palace shining like a beacon in the distance. *"Find Father and tell him I've found the blue pearl. Let him know I'm safe and on my way to find Halla."*

"All right," Toren replies.

My father's voice fills my mind. *"My son, I would speak with you before you leave."*

I stop short and then follow Toren as we go to him. We find him alone in his throne room. *"What is it, Father?"*

He swims to us, placing a hand on each of our shoulders.

"Thank the gods you are back safely." His expression sobers as his gaze drops to the blue pearl necklace. *"You are sure this is what you want?"*

"I am," I reply without hesitation.

"I worry for you, you know. I know that, at times, I have been... hard on you, but it is only because I wanted the best for you, my son."

I swallow against the lump in my throat. *"I know, Father."*

"After your mother died, you and Toren were all I had. You are my greatest treasures, my two sons," he says. *"You really mean to go through with this? To bind her to you if she regains her memories and agrees to take you as her mate?"*

"Yes."

I'm surprised when he throws his arms around me and Toren, hugging us tight.

"It will not be an easy life, my son," he whispers in my mind.

"I know. But I cannot live without her. She is my heart, Father—she is my fated one."

"Then, go with my blessing," he says. *"Hurry. She is set to bond with King Henrick this night, on his ship. The ceremony will start soon."*

Panic tightens my chest as I swim toward Solwyck. My tail cannot propel me fast enough as I race through the water. I have to stop her wedding.

She cannot bond with King Henrick. She is mine.

When I break through the surface of the water, I cast my gaze to the shoreline in the far distance. Several softly glowing lights line the beach near the castle. The entire city itself seems lit in a vibrant display.

My heart stutters and stops when I notice the lights are lined up from the castle down to Henrick's ship, docked in the harbor. Several bouquets of flowers and ribbons decorate his ship.

I lift my eyes to the dark sky and the full blue moon overhead, praying I am not too late.

My pulse pounds in my ears as I make my way to the ship. As soon as I reach it, I call up to the deck, hoping someone will hear me. "Is anyone there?"

"Aye!" a voice calls back.

A moment later, a male looks over the deck toward the water. His blue eyes pierce mine. "Are you in some kind of trouble?"

"King Henrick and Princess Halla… where are they?"

He turns toward the castle. "They're at the palace."

"Thank you," I say quickly and then dive beneath the water, swimming as fast as I can to the castle, desperate to find Halla. I have to stop her before she marries Henrick.

She is mine. My mate—my fated one. Not his. He will not love her as I do. He will not thank the gods each and every night because he has her by his side.

She is everything to me and I cannot lose her.

My pulse pounds in my ears as I make my way to the palace. I pray I'm not too late.

CHAPTER 31

HALLA

I sit in front of the mirror as Althea runs a comb through my long, red hair. Dressed in my silken, white wedding gown, I stare at my reflection, trying to convince myself this is what I want, when I know, deep down that it's not.

Gerold walks into my room. "You are sure you want to go through with this?" he asks.

I sigh and turn toward him. "Henrick is a good man. He may be blunt, but he is honest, and kind and—" I stop short. Drawing in a deep breath, I meet Gerold's eyes evenly. In my heart, I know this is wrong. I do not love him. "I cannot marry him. Oh, Gerold, what have I done? He is a good person. I do not want to shame him and—"

Gerold gives me a faint smile and kisses my forehead. "As you said, he is a good man. And an honest one. He appreciates the truth, and he will respect your decision. I'm sure of it."

He hugs me and pulls Althea into the embrace. "I'll call him in here to speak with you. All right?"

I nod.

It doesn't take long for Henrick to come to my room. As soon as he enters, he walks toward me. He takes my hand and sits down in a chair beside me. "You have changed your mind."

He says this as a statement, but I recognize it is also a question. "Yes."

His blue eyes study me a moment before speaking. "Thank you for being honest." He darts a glance at my brother. "Our alliance will remain intact either way. Whatever aid your city needs, you must simply ask, and it is yours."

Gently, I squeeze his hand and his gaze snaps back to mine. "You are a good and honorable man, Henrick. Thank you for understanding."

A faint smile crests his lips. "If you change your mind, my offer still stands."

Guilt fills me. "I… do not want to offer you any false hope, Henrick. I have made my decision."

He grins. "You cannot blame me for trying, can you?"

"No," I laugh softly. "I suppose not."

He stands. "Well, I suppose I will be off."

"Surely, you do not mean to sail away tonight. It would be safer to leave in the morning, would it not?" Gerold calls from the doorway. "You are welcome to stay as long as you like."

"I appreciate that," he says. "I will take you up on your offer and stay tonight. I will leave at dawn."

He makes his way to the balcony, casting his gaze out to the sea.

I carefully make my way to his side.

My mouth drifts open as I notice a pair of glowing blue eyes staring up at me from the water.

"A Mer," Henrick murmurs beside me, pointing at him.

"Halla!" the Merman calls out.

"Who are you?" I reply. "How do you know my name?"

"Please," he replies. "Meet me down at the shoreline."

Henrick growls low in his throat, and Gerold moves to stand on my other side. "What do you want with my sister?" he shouts.

"I just wish to speak with her. That is all."

"Come to me, Halla," a voice seems to whisper on the wind, tugging at my very soul as if there was an invisible tether between us. *"Please. You must trust me."*

I feel compelled to go to him. As if this is the reason I am drawn to the sea.

"Fate led us to each other," I remember the whispered words of the man in my dreams.

While I understand it is strange, I cannot ignore this feeling. I must go to the shoreline. I look to Henrick and Gerold. "Will you help me down?"

Gerold's head jerks back. "You wish to speak with him?"

"Yes."

He frowns and I take his hand. "I… cannot explain it, Gerold, but there is something familiar about him. I have to talk to him. I need to understand why I feel this way." I dart a glance to the sea. "I have dreamed of those eyes. Several times. It's as if I know him somehow."

Gerold blinks several times, but finally nods in agreement. "Fine. But I will go with you."

"I'll come as well," Henrick says, his voice a low growl. "If he dares try to drag you into the water, I will end him."

"I do not think he wants to hurt me," I say quickly.

"How do you know?" Henrick's gaze snaps to mine. "He is Mer. There are rumors about them, you know."

"Yes, but their people helped ours. They gave us several chests full of treasure to rebuild the city. I doubt they want to harm any of us."

He sighs. "I suppose you are right. But still… you cannot be too careful."

Still dressed in my wedding gown, I make my way through the castle. Henrick on one arm and Gerold on the other.

My progress is slow and my legs feel weak, but I refuse to give up, even as Gerold and Henrick offer to carry me the rest of the way to the beach.

Instead, I continue out into the gardens and down the pathway to the shoreline.

When we reach the beach, the waves crash upon the shore. The warm water washes over my feet and ankles, leaving trails of seafoam in the sand as it retreats.

My hair whips around me as the cool air blows in off the sea.

A Merman swims toward us and my mouth drifts open as I recognize the man from my dreams.

CHAPTER 32

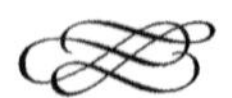

ERRIK

Carefully, she makes her way down to the shoreline. A low growl rumbles my chest when I notice Henrick beside her and her arm looped through his.

She is dressed in a long, white gown that I recognize as the clothing that humans wear for their bonding ceremonies. My chest tightens for I fear that I am too late. That they are already wed.

Her long, silken red hair blows softly in the wind behind her. It is pinned up in an intricate series of twists and braids and secured with several pearls. My eyes widen as I take in her lovely form. She is even more beautiful, up close, than I had remembered.

Her steps are slow and a bit unsteady, but I smile as I notice the determination etched in her features as she releases her grip on Henrick and her brother, and continues across the beach on her own.

I swim close to the shore. The moment her eyes meet

mine, she inhales sharply.

"Your eyes... I know them."

"Please." I swallow against the knot of worry in my stomach. "Tell me you are not yet married."

"I'm not," she replies.

Relief moves through me. I clasp my hand around the blue pearl and speak clearly. "Remember me, Halla. Remember our love. You are my heart, and I am yours."

The pearl begins to glow in my palm. The soft blue light extending a long tendril toward Halla. I watch, stunned as it wraps around her form.

Her brother and Henrick start toward her but stop abruptly as it disappears. Her lips curve up in a stunning smile and she starts toward me. "Errik!"

I drag myself out of the water and she drops to her knees in the sand. I gather her in my arms and run my fingers through her long, scarlet hair as I stare deep into her lovely blue eyes. "Halla," I breathe out her name like a prayer.

She cups my cheek. "What happened?"

I press a series of tender kisses to her cheeks, brow and nose. I'm so thankful to have her again in my arms. "My beautiful, Halla, you made a deal with a blood witch to save my life. In exchange, you sacrificed your memories and your love for me. But I have found a way to restore them."

A tear slides down her cheek. "I remember now, my love."

I crush my lips to hers in a branding kiss. "Oh, Halla," I breathe between kisses. "I was so afraid I was too late. That you'd already bound yourself to another."

"Errik," she whispers against my lips. "I almost lost you, my love."

Tears sting my eyes, but I blink them back. "You saved me, Halla."

She traces her fingers along my torso, over the jagged scar of my injury. "I remember," she whispers. "I went to the blood witch and made a bargain to save your life." She looks back at Henrick. "Henrick helped me."

He dips his chin in a subtle nod, and when his eyes meet mine, they narrow. "You best treat her well, or the two of us will have a problem."

Gerold gives me a stern look as he gestures to Henrick. "I second what he said."

Halla laughs softly—the sound light and airy, almost musical in quality. It has been so long since I've heard it.

Together, they start back up the beach, leaving us alone.

I pull her into my lap and cup her cheek as I capture her mouth again with my own. I cannot stop touching her. "I have missed you. So very much. You are my heart, and I love you, Halla. With all that I am. I desire more than anything to bind you to me. Please, my beloved, will you take me as your mate?"

A stunning smile curves her lips, and she kisses me passionately. She curls her tongue around mine, deepening our kiss. "Yes." She smiles against my lips. "I will be yours, and you will be mine, Errik."

I thread my fingers through her hair, gripping the long, soft red strands and tipping her head back as I seal my mouth over hers in a claiming kiss.

CHAPTER 33

HALLA

Errik claims my mouth in a passionate kiss, leaving me breathless and panting. He pulls me close and swims us out toward the rock formation and the small island that we consider ours.

Instead of going up onto the beach, he remains in the water. He wraps his strong arms even tighter around me, and pushes me back against one of the rocks.

I wrap my legs around his waist and twine my arms around his neck, gently running my fingers through the hair at the nape of his neck as his gaze meets mine, full of desire and possession.

His stav is a hard bar between us; only a thin scrap of silken material separating him from my entrance. "I want you, Halla. I long to claim you as mine. But I will not make love to you if you do not—"

I press a finger to his lips to silence him. "I want you, Errik. More than anything."

His glowing blue eyes hold mine with a possessive gaze. He uses his claws and tears away my silken undergarment.

He cups my cheek and presses his lips to mine. His hand travels down my neck to the valley of my breasts. He tugs at the neckline of my dress, freeing my breasts and cupping one in his palm.

A low moan escapes me as he brushes his thumb across the already sensitive peak.

"You are perfect," he whispers against my lips.

He positions the crown of his stav at my entrance. His nostrils flare, and his pupils dilate until only a thin rim of glowing blue is visible around the edges.

"You are mine, Halla."

The bright moonlight affords me just enough light that I can make out the details of his body. My mouth drifts open when I glance beneath the water to his stav extending from his mating pouch. With his pointed ears, glowing blue eyes, sharp fangs, and dark claws, he is terrifyingly beautiful, but I am not afraid.

"I long to claim you as my mate. Will you accept me?"

"Yes."

My heart pounds as his gaze holds mine, the breath stuttering from my lungs as he slowly enters me.

Tight heat blooms in my core as he breaks through my barrier. He rolls his hips back and forth, slowly advancing. He's so large that, at first, everything is tight and uncomfortable as he sheathes himself deep inside me.

I've never felt so full. When he shifts his hips, everything changes. The pain disappears and is replaced by only pleasure.

We stare at one another in mutual wonder at the feeling of our bodies joined together as he strokes deep inside me.

He groans as I wrap my legs around him. "So tight," he rasps.

My fingers trace over his powerful form. The strong muscles of his tail undulating beneath my hands as he pumps into me. Each stroke becoming longer, deeper and more forceful.

My head falls back and my lips part on a moan as sensation overwhelms me. I've never felt so full, and I love the delicious friction of his stav moving deep inside me.

He cups my breast, rolling the sensitive peak between his thumb and forefinger, careful of his claws as he touches me.

I arch up into his hand. "More," I breathe.

Something unleashes inside him. He wraps his arms tighter around me, pinning me between him and the rock. I always knew he was strong, but as he thrusts into me, I finally understand the full extent of his strength as his powerful form moves beneath my hands as they trace over his back and down his tail.

His breath is warm in my ear as he groans. "You are mine, Halla."

The muscles of my channel beginning to flex and quiver around his length. Pleasure coils deep in my core. I'm so close to the edge.

A slight twinge of pain deep inside me turns quickly into pleasure, and I gasp as warmth blooms in my core. My toes curl with pleasure. "What is that?" I barely manage.

"My stem," he groans. "It extends from the tip of my stav to enter your womb and fill you with my seed."

The sensation is so intense, my body tightens around him. Each thrust becomes longer and deeper.

His name escapes my lips as a soft moan. I'm so close to the edge.

His gaze holds mine, fierce and possessive. He growls and the vibration moves straight through me, and I fall over the edge into my climax. Wave after wave of pleasure washes through me as I cling to him and cry out his name.

My release triggers his, and he roars, "Mine!"

An intense burst of warmth erupts deep inside me, filling me with an endless rush of delicious heat. It triggers another orgasm, this one even more intense than the last, and I cry out his name as pleasure fills me so great I can barely contain it.

I'm not even recovered from my orgasm when he begins to move inside me again. His eyes search mine. "I must have you again, Halla. Do you accept me?"

I wrap my arms around him. "Always."

When we have finished making love for the second time, he pulls us up onto the beach. Just when I think we're finished, he positions his tip at my entrance and groans low in his throat as he pushes into me again.

My eyes roll to the back of my head at the delicious stretch as he sheathes himself deep in my core.

He takes me slowly this time, his eyes staring deep into mine as he strokes into me. Another small twinge of pain turns into intense pleasure and I arch up against him as his stem enters my womb.

As he continues to move deep inside me, it doesn't take long before I'm close to the edge once more.

My head falls back as a low moan escapes my lips. "Errik," I breathe out his name.

He grips my chin. "I want to watch you as you come," he growls.

His gaze holds mine as his lips pull back in an almost feral snarl. He quickens his pace until he is pumping into me. My body tenses like a bowstring, and I fall over the edge into complete and glorious oblivion. He roars as warmth blooms in my core, and he fills me again with his essence.

We both pant heavily as we come down from our release. He captures my mouth in a branding kiss and breathes against my lips, "You are mine."

CHAPTER 34

HALLA

I stand on the beach facing Errik. Sitting atop one of the rocks, he takes my hand in his as the priest performs our ceremony. People gather around us on the beach, while several Mer, including Errik's father and brother watch from the water as we recite our vows.

I place a wreath of shells and flowers atop Errik's head and he does the same to me. His mouth curves up in a devastatingly handsome smile as he speaks the words aloud. "You are mine, and I am yours."

"I am yours," I repeat to him. "And you are mine."

He captures my mouth in a claiming kiss as everyone around us cheers.

It is the last night of the blue moon cycle. It's been almost two weeks since my memory returned and I've never been happier. Errik pulls himself up over the balcony of my room.

It's our wedding night, so I am still dressed in my wedding gown as I greet him.

His gaze travels down my form appreciatively. "You are stunning," he whispers. "And all mine."

The soft moonlight illuminates his features. I trace my fingers lightly over the pointed tip of his left ear and then move down the chiseled planes of muscle that line his abdomen and chest. The scales of his body like silk beneath my hands. When I reach his tail, I marvel at the softly glowing blue color of his scales.

I know he's strong, but it still surprises me when he gathers me to his chest with one arm and drags himself, while holding me up, to the bed.

He moves over me and presses a tender kiss to my lips. He pulls back and uses his claws to tear a line down my wedding dress, removing it from my body and leaving me bare beneath him.

His gaze travels over my form, full of fire and possession.

I watch as his stav extends from his body, full and erect.

I wrap my hand around him, feeling the slickness that coats the scales from the several small bumps along the shaft. A bead of blue liquid forms on the tip as I open myself to him.

"You are beautiful, Halla," he whispers softly as he positions himself at my entrance.

My lips part on a moan as he slowly enters me.

"You feel so good," he groans as he begins to move deep inside me.

I cup the back of his neck and bring his lips down to mine, curling my tongue around his and deepening our kiss as he pumps into me.

The slight twinge as his stem enters my womb is quickly replaced by pleasure.

Nothing exists outside of this moment between us and the movements of his body against mine.

I move my hands down his back, feeling the powerful muscles of his form with each flex of his hips as he thrusts into me.

The friction of his stav deep in my core is so intense, my head falls back as a low moan escapes me.

He cups my chin, forcing my gaze to his, and growls low in his throat. "I want to watch you as you come."

His glowing blue eyes never leave mine as he thrusts into me. My body tightens around him and then I'm coming harder than I ever have before.

Delicious heat erupts deep inside me and warmth blooms in my core as he roars my name, filling me with his seed.

When I wake in the morning, we're tangled in the sheets. My inner thighs are sticky with his release. My cheeks heat when I notice the deep blue color staining my skin and the bedding.

I pull back the covers slightly, and gasp when I notice that instead of a tail, Errik's two legs are brushing against mine.

"Errik!"

His eyes snap open and follow my gaze. He inhales sharply, staring at his legs in wonder. "How is this possible?"

"I… do not know."

His legs are heavily muscled and covered in blue scales. I gently run my fingers over them, marveling at this miracle.

I change, and he covers himself with a sheet even though his mating pouch is still intact, hiding his stav from sight. I call for Althea, and when she enters, her eyes widen as they travel over his form. He stands in the middle of the bedroom on two human legs.

Her eyes dart to the necklace he always wears. "The blue pearl." She smiles. "It worked."

He blinks. "You knew this would happen?"

"I hoped, but I was not sure."

"Dorin mentioned Mer used to seek blue pearls for this reason, but why now? Why did this not happen when Halla first regained her memory?"

She shrugs. "I do not know. Last night was the end of the blue moon cycle. Perhaps it is somehow tied to that."

He licks his lips, considering. "Will I remain this way?"

"There is only one way to be sure," she replies. "We must go down to the ocean."

She sends the guards to retrieve my brother. As soon as he enters, his jaw drops. "How did—"

"The Blue Pearl, I suspect," Althea answers.

My brother quickly retrieves a shirt and pants for Errik. As we walk through the castle, Errik is somehow able to move as if he has always had legs. Whereas, I struggle still to coordinate my movements as I walk with one arm looped through Gerold's and another through Errik's.

Our guards all watch wide-eyed but say nothing as we pass. When we reach the ocean, Althea instructs Errik to walk into the water.

Toren's head peeks above the surface. His jaw drops. "What happened to you?"

Errik smiles. "I do not know. Isn't it wonderful?"

He arches a brow. "No, you look like a human." His eyes dart to me. "Forgive me, I meant no disrespect."

I laugh. "None taken."

Errik wades into the water, and in an instant, his legs are replaced by his gorgeous blue tail. He flips up his fin to show us, but I notice the concern in his expression as he faces Althea. "Is it gone? Am I stuck as a Mer again forever?"

She shakes her head. "Come back out, and we'll know."

He drags himself out of the water completely. His pants are gone, ripped from the transformation, but his borrowed shirt covers his waist down to his thighs. We watch in awe as his tail splits back into two human legs.

He stands and rushes toward me, pulling me into his arms and spinning me around in a slow circle. He captures my mouth in a claiming kiss. "I can live in your world, Halla," he whispers against my lips. "We can make a life anywhere you wish."

I smile and dart a glance at my brother. "Then, let us continue to live by the sea. After all, someone has to take care of Gerold."

Gerold laughs and embraces us warmly, pulling Althea into the hug as well. "I would like that," he says. "I would like that very much."

Errik looks to Toren. "And Toren cannot do without me either."

Toren rolls his eyes, but I do not miss the smile that tugs at the corner of his lips.

EPILOGUE

HALLA

We wait anxiously in the throne room for the Fae Prince Ryvan and his human wife, Princess Ella, to arrive. They have come with their royal Fae Healer to see if they can help me.

I've reached a plateau in my recovery. I'm able to walk, but it is still only for short distances and not without great difficulty. Sometimes the pain in my legs becomes so great that I have to use my chair. I am grateful that I can walk, but I wish desperately to regain the full use of my legs.

One of the guards enters, interrupting our conversation. He bows low. "Forgive the intrusion, Your Highnesses," he announces. "Prince Ryvan and Princess Ella have arrived."

My heart slams in my throat. I push my hands into my lap to still their shaking as I tip my chin up, ready to receive our most welcome guests. I'm anxious to meet them, but nervous that my hopes are for naught. I so desperately want to regain the full use of my legs.

"Show them in," Gerold orders.

The doors open, and my mouth drifts open when the prince and princess appear. They are indeed a handsome pair. He has dark hair, glowing green eyes, and the pointed ears typical of his kin, lending him an ethereal handsomeness that human men could never achieve. A ghost of a smile crests my lips, for not even this Fae can rival Errik's attractiveness. I take his hand in mine, squeezing gently.

The princess has chestnut hair that frames her shoulders. Her eyes are pale blue, like a clear sky on a warm day. Her face is heart-shaped, and I smile when I realize she has freckles, just like me and my brother.

I'm still slightly stunned that she is human. Ryvan's father sealed the borders of their kingdom with magic shortly after Ryvan's mother was killed by an invading human army. He hated humans, and I wonder how Ryvan and Ella fell in love in the first place. I make a mental note to ask her when we are alone later.

My brother stands to greet them. "Welcome, Prince Ryvan and Princess Ella. I am King Gerold, and this is my sister, Princess Halla, and her husband, Prince Errik. We are glad you have arrived safely."

Prince Ryvan inclines his head. "Thank you. We are happy to be here." His eyes dart to me, and I'm struck by the kindness they express. "We only hope that our Healer may be of help to the princess."

He glances over his shoulder, and another Fae steps into the light. His eyes glow light blue, and his hair is the color of spun gold. He bows to us. "I am Healer Oradon."

I smile. "I have been eagerly awaiting your arrival. Thank you very much for coming to offer aid."

Princess Ella addresses me. "As soon as we heard you needed help, we knew we had to come. Our kingdom knows of your bravery, Princess. We only hope that we will be able to help you."

"You may call me Halla," I tell her, nodding in acknowledgment.

She flashes a dazzling smile. "Then you may call me Ella."

I like them already.

~

We all head to the dining hall, offering our guests food after their long journey. Ella sits beside me, Errik and Ryvan are seated across from us, and my brother sits at the head of the table. I cannot help but notice Ryvan lovingly place his hand over Ella's slightly swollen abdomen when she settles.

I glance down at her stomach. "You are with child?"

"Yes." Her face is practically glowing. "A girl."

"How lovely." I smile, my hand alighting over my abdomen as well.

"You are, too?" she asks.

I nod, trying to keep my expression cheerful despite my fears.

Healer Oradon tilts his head. "Forgive me. May I interject?" His gaze darts to Errik. "I understand you are Mer—is that correct?"

Errik nods.

Oradon frowns. "You are worried because you fear the child was conceived when you were in that form."

My mouth drifts open. "How did you know?"

"Oradon is a seer," Ryvan says.

"I believe the child will be Mer, but I will have to assess you to be certain."

Panic stops my heart. "Please," I ask anxiously. "Can you examine me now?"

He nods and stands from his chair. Approaching, he takes my hand. He closes his eyes and lowers his head, features tensing in deep concentration. After a moment, he tips his head back up to me and smiles.

"I was right; your daughter will be like her father. Both will live in two worlds. So will any future children conceived of your union."

Relief floods me, so great I feel as if my heart will burst. Gerold and Althea beam and I've never been happier.

~

Later that night, as we lie in bed, tangled up in each other's arms, Errik places his hand lovingly over my abdomen. "Our daughter will be able to spend time with both our families."

I comb my fingers through his hair, capturing his glowing blue eyes. "You can show her where you came from and teach her about the sea."

He kisses me, smiling against my lips. "More importantly, her uncle Toren can watch her whenever her parents need some time alone." I laugh, but he sobers. "How do your legs feel?"

"About the same, maybe a little better. I have regained more feeling, and when Oradon used his magic, they seemed… stronger somehow. It's too soon to know for sure, though."

He cups my face. "And if they remain as they are?"

I know he asks because he worries I'll fall into depression. Yet the truth is, I've never been more content. I touch his cheek then trace the pointed tip of his ear as I stare deep into his eyes.

"Even if I never fully heal, I do not need this to be happy, Errik. I have you and our daughter. You are all I need, my love."

His eyes brighten with tears as he cups my cheek. He brushes his lips to mine and whispers against them. "You are my heart, Halla." Tenderly, he splays his palm across my abdomen. "Fate led us to each other, and I will always be yours."

ALSO BY JESSICA GRAYSON

Next book in the series - ***Bound To The Elf Prince: A Snow White Retelling***

If you enjoyed this book, please leave a review on Amazon and/or Goodreads.

If you want to King Henrick's story, his book is available as well. ***Claimed By The Bear King: A Snow Queen Retelling***

Jessica Grayson also writes under the pen name Aria Winter

Want more Fairy Tale Retellings?

Once Upon a Fairy Tale Romance Series

Taken by the Dragon: A Beauty and the Beast Retelling

Captivated by the Fae: A Cinderella Retelling

Rescued By The Merman: A Little Mermaid Retelling

Bound To The Elf Prince: A Snow White Retelling

Claimed By The Bear King: A Snow Queen Retelling

Protected By The Wolf Prince: A Red Riding Hood Retelling

Of Fate and Kings Series (Fantasy Romance Standalone Series)

Bound to the Dark Elf King

Claimed by the Dragon King

Taken by the Fae King

Stolen by the Wolf King

Captured by the Orc King

Of Gods and Fate (Greek God Romance Standalone Fantasy/Paranormal series)

Claimed By Hades

Bound to Ares

Orc Claimed Series (Fantasy Romance Standalone Series)

Claimed by the Orc

Of Dragons and Elves Series (Fantasy Romance)

The Elf Knight

Scarred Dragon Prince Series (Fantasy Romance)

Shadow Guard: Dragon Shifter Romance

To Love a Monster Book Series (Fantasy Romance)

Claimed by the Monster: A Monster Romance

Ice World Warrior Series (Scifi Romance)

Claimed: Dragon Shifter Romance

Bound: Vampire Alien Romance

Rescued: Fae Alien Romance

Stolen: Werewolf Romance

Taken: Vampire Alien Romance

Fated: Dragon Shifter Romance

Protected: Dragon Shifter Romance

Chosen: Vampire Alien Romance

Want Dragon Shifters? You can dive into their world with this completed Duology.

Mosauran Series (Dragon Shifter Alien Romance)

The Edge of it All

Shape of the Wind

V'loryn Series (Vampire Alien Romance)

Lost in the Deep End

Beneath a Different Sky

Under a Silver Moon

V'loryn Holiday Series (A Marek and Elizabeth Holiday novella takes place prior to their bonding)

The Thing We Choose

V'loryn Fated Ones (Vampire Alien Romance)

Where the Light Begins (Vanek's Story)

Settlers of the Outer Rim Series (Scifi Romance)

Rescued: Fox Shifter Romance

Protected: Lizard Man Romance

For information about upcoming releases Like me on

Facebook at Jessica Grayson

http://facebook.com/JessicaGraysonBooks.

OR

sign up for upcoming release alerts at my website:

Jessicagraysonauthor.com

Printed in Great Britain
by Amazon